SONGS IN THE SILENCE

By the same author

ALICE DODD AND THE SPIRIT OF TRUTH

Catherine Frey Murphy

SONGS IN THE SILENCE

Macmillan Publishing Company
New York

Maxwell Macmillan Canada
Toronto

Maxwell Macmillan International
New York   Oxford   Singapore   Sydney

ACKNOWLEDGMENTS

This book was made possible in part by a grant from the Society of Children's Book Writers and Illustrators. For research help, I would also like to thank the New England Aquarium; the Library of Natural Sounds of the Cornell Laboratory of Ornithology; the Rogers Environmental Center of Sherburne, New York; the Portland Public Library; and the public libraries of New York State.

For the sake of my story, I have taken some liberties with the geography of Casco Bay. Garnet Island, Maine General Hospital, Lighthouse Hill, Harborside Middle School, and the Jewel Islands are imaginary places, and no character in the book bears any intentional resemblance to any real person, living or dead.

Library of Congress Cataloging-in-Publication Data
Murphy, Catherine Frey.
  Songs in the silence / by Catherine Frey Murphy. — 1st ed.   p.   cm.
  Summary: Having found a mental link with the two whales that have entered the harbor of her Maine island, eleven-year-old Hallie hopes both to save them and to use their healing power to help her hospitalized younger brother.
  ISBN 0-02-767730-3
  [1. Whales—Fiction. 2. Human-animal communication—Fiction. 3. Wildlife rescue—Fiction. 4. Maine—Fiction. 5. Islands—Fiction. 6. Brothers and sisters—Fiction.] I. Title.
  PZ7.M9523So 1994   [Fic]—dc20   93-26947

For Tom

But far on the deep there are billows,
That never shall break on the beach;
And I have heard songs in the Silence
That never shall float into speech.

—ABRAM JOSEPH RYAN

PROLOGUE

In the middle of the night before the accident, the last night we were all together, before everything changed, my little brother, Josh, came thumping into my bed, shaking me awake. He burrowed under the covers beside me, crowding close. I could feel his wiry body shivering.

"What's up, Joshie?" I murmured, too sleepy to open my eyes.

"A monkey came out of my ceiling." His whisper was loud and frightened in the dark. "It was big, Hallie."

I forced my eyes open. By the dim hall light I could just see his freckled face. "Joshie, it was a dream," I told him. "You had a nightmare. There aren't really any monkeys in your room."

He stared at me, unconvinced, his bony knees poking into my stomach, his bad dream still a menacing shadow in his eyes. Sleepily, I slid over to make room for him, so that I was balanced uncomfortably on the edge of the mattress. My bed wasn't big enough for two people, even when one of us was only six years old.

"Just a bad dream, Josh," I repeated. "You made it up in your own head. No monkeys, I promise. Come on, let me take you back to your own bed now."

But at that, his arms wound tight around my neck, and he dug his head in hard against my chest.

I sighed. "Okay, okay, you can stay with me. But just this once." I crossed my eyes at him. That made him smile, and he stuck out his tongue at me. Then, with his arms still wrapped around my neck, he relaxed, and before long he was snoring. His hair tickled my nose.

Josh was so noisy and full of beans in the daytime that, soft with sleep in my bed, he was like an entirely different brother, cuddly and warm and quiet. But it was hard to get back to sleep, teetering on the edge of my bed with his bony arms under my head. I lay awake listening to his soft breathing for a long time before I finally drifted off.

Now I'm the one who has bad dreams, who comes up gasping out of sleep, trying to make myself move, to shake off the immobility that keeps me frozen, stops me from catching my brother, beating at the fire, putting out the flames licking up the legs of his jeans.

But Josh isn't here. He isn't in my bed, and he's not in his own bed, either. He isn't even here on the island. He's in Maine General Hospital on the mainland, with my mother, where they're treating his burned leg. And so I come awake alone, my heart pounding, without even the sweet realization that it was only a dream. Because it wasn't; this nightmare was real. I lie there in the dark, remembering that it's too late now to make myself move, too late to put out the fire.

If Josh wakes up in the hospital with a bad dream, I won't be there. And when I wake up from my own bad dreams, the worst dreams I've ever had, he isn't here for me. I have to lie here alone, listening to the creaking of our empty house and to the ocean muttering against the rocks outside, whispering into the dark, "I'm sorry. Oh, Joshie, I'm so sorry."

SONGS IN THE SILENCE

1

"I'm lost." Hallie pushed a strand of fog-damp hair out of her eyes. "I don't know how to get back to shore. And I'm not even sure I care."

Hallie's dinghy rose and fell, rose and fell, on the gray water. Mist lay thick around her, blending with the soft silver of the sea, so that the island shore she had pushed off from only a moment before was gone as completely as if it had never been there at all. The beach, the cove, the other islands, the city of Portland just across the harbor, had disappeared, and Hallie and her dinghy floated alone in a new, small, muffled world, made entirely of mist.

Small waves lapped at the wooden boat, and the wail of a lone gull sliced through the mist. Foghorns moaned across the bay, a low lament in mournful voices, like lost dinosaurs endlessly searching for each other.

There had been no fog when Hallie got into the boat. At sunrise, when she had climbed quietly out her window and slid down the shed roof to slip away from her house, a bank of gray clouds had hung low over the ocean off-shore, but the sky over the island had been clear.

The cove had been quiet when she ran down the

wooden steps onto the beach, the only person there so early on a September morning. The sand had been cold and damp under her bare feet. She'd seen Mr. Gianopoulos's dinghy pulled up above the tide line on the sand, its blue-painted plank seats bare and inviting. It had looked to her like a good place to sit and think, a good place to cry.

She hadn't cried yet, not once since Josh got hurt. She had come to the beach in search of privacy, wanting to get away from home, away from her father, away from the constant, aching absence of her mother and her brother, away from everything. But when she climbed into the dinghy and sat down, she found she couldn't let go and cry.

Somebody might see her. Somebody might come along the beach, even so early in the day—a jogger out for a run, or a fisherman hoping for an early catch, or a child eager to skip stones across the gentle water of the cove. Somebody might spot her, a ridiculous sight, an eleven-year-old girl with uncombed hair, nose red, eyes streaming, bare feet blue with cold, sitting in a rowboat sniffling, right out in the middle of the beach.

But on the water, nobody would catch her crying. Out there, nobody would see a thing. Suddenly determined, Hallie had climbed back out of the dinghy and untied it from its metal mooring sunk in the rocks. She had shoved it fiercely across the damp sand and waded, pushing the boat ahead of her, out into the icy water of the cove until the dinghy bobbed free in the foamy shallows. Then she had climbed in and pushed off.

It wasn't until the boat had floated well away from the

beach that it occurred to Hallie to wonder how she would get back. She wasn't very good at rowing, and she didn't know how to use the battered old outboard motor fastened to the stern. Her best friend, Melissa, whose father owned this dinghy, had always done the rowing when the two of them had taken it out before. Melissa was a lobsterman's daughter, as comfortable in boats as she was on land. Because of Melissa, Hallie had never needed to learn much about handling boats.

The only other boat Hallie had spent much time in was the ferryboat that carried her back and forth between the city of Portland and the island. It was so big and square and solid that it was more like a city bus than a boat. She wasn't much of a swimmer, either. She could make it once across the warm, chlorinated width of the YWCA pool if she had to, but the cold Maine waters around Garnet Island were something else.

But Hallie had thought she could manage to row back to shore somehow, when she was ready. It wasn't far; the cove was small and sheltered, its water quiet. The Barrier Rocks scattered across the mouth of the cove made a kind of interrupted wall, protecting it from the deep, rough water of the open ocean beyond.

The dinghy had bobbed gently, comfortingly, in the quiet waves, as if it were rocking her. Hallie had taken a deep breath, put her damp, salty hands up to her face, and waited for the tears to spill over at last.

That was when the fog rolled in. It swept in from the sea and fell around the boat, as suddenly as a curtain dropping on a stage. Sky, sea, and shore all disappeared, and Hallie was alone.

For a moment she couldn't understand what had happened. It seemed as if her feelings had taken on a thick, damp life of their own. Already her face was so wet from the mist that she couldn't tell what dampness came from the fog and what from the few tears that had had time to slide down her cheeks. She shoved an impatient hand roughly over her eyes, trying uselessly to clear the fog away so that she could see better while she figured out what to do.

She was still in the cove, still somewhere near the shore. But she wasn't far from the Barrier Rocks, where the water grew rough and treacherous. Even Melissa wouldn't take the dinghy near the Barrier Rocks in the fog. And if she drifted through the gaps among the rocks, she would find herself on the open ocean, out where the surf smashed against the boulders of the backshore, where the high, steel prows of oil tankers plowed through the waves toward Portland, ready to run her down.

I'll just have to row back to shore, thought Hallie. Right now, while I can still remember which way to go. She gathered up the oars, heavy and unfamiliar in her hands, and tried to remember how Melissa did it. Melissa always sat backward in the boat, rowing with swift, sure strokes, glancing confidently over her shoulder now and then to see where she was going, trusting the boat and the water and her own strong, brown arms. Melissa made rowing look easy.

But when Hallie tried it, the oars battled with her, splashing and slipping away, spattering cold water onto her damp face and her shirt. They slipped fast along the surface instead of pulling deep in the water, so that the boat went nowhere. Or one pulled deep while the other skittered out, spinning the dinghy sideways, leaving Hallie disoriented, not sure anymore which way lay the beach. The oars creaked in their oarlocks, a screeching protest, as if they knew that Hallie was not their master.

Hallie struggled until she was breathless and the palms of her hands were sore, but there was still no sign of the shore, and the fog was an impenetrable wall on all sides. Even if she could manage to get the boat to go, she couldn't tell anymore which was the right direction. At last she dropped the oars into the bottom of the boat.

"I'll just have to wait for it to lift," she said aloud. She could feel the fog flow into her mouth when she spoke, damp and gray like thin cotton. The foghorns moaned beyond the mist, the only reminder of the larger world. The swells under the dinghy were growing larger. She was afraid she was drifting toward the mouth of the cove.

If this were a story, Hallie thought, somebody would rescue me, a lobsterman or a dog or some kind of hero. But it wasn't a story, it was real life. Nobody knew where she was, and nobody would come to the beach in the fog. Even if she yelled for help, there was nobody close enough to hear. Nobody was going to rescue her.

After all, no hero had come along for Josh. Nobody had rescued him. Not even Hallie, and that was the worst part, because maybe she could have kept him from being hurt, if she had acted in time. She had been the first one to hear him, from down on the beach where he was supposed to be with Hallie and Melissa and their families, watching the Round-the-Island Boat Race. His screaming, too thin, too high, too scared, had pulled her away from the race, up the steps to the top of the bluff, over the path to her yard.

But when she had seen Josh, running away from the overturned barbecue grill, the grass around the grill on fire, his pants just starting to flame, Hallie had frozen. She hadn't been able to move at all.

It had been Melissa's mother who moved. After what had seemed like forever but was probably only a few seconds, Mrs. Gianopoulos had run past Hallie from the beach. She had knocked Josh down and beat out his fiery pants with her hands. And then Hallie's mother and father had come, and then a lot of other people, and finally, Hallie had been able to move again, to go to Josh, to hold his hand while they waited for the ambulance. But by then, of course, it was too late; Josh was already burned. Hallie closed her eyes against the memory, but that only made the terrible pictures clearer in her brain.

"I don't care." She spoke out loud again. "I don't even want to be rescued."

It was just after she spoke that the rowboat hit the first rock. She felt it before she heard it, a gentle jar and then a scrape against the worn boards of the dinghy floor, a grating groan like the lonely moan of the foghorns. The dinghy lurched and shuddered, but then a swell came, a slow rising of the water that lifted the dinghy over the rock and free again into the waves.

Hallie jerked one oar loose from its oarlock and poked it frantically into the water, hanging on to it with both hands, peering around her into the dense fog. The waves were definitely bigger. She had drifted into the Barrier

Rocks. Were there more rocks nearby? There must be, but she couldn't see.

The oar struck another rock, or maybe it was the same one. Hallie braced the oar against it and shoved hard. The boat slid away sideways, like a crab. Then there was another thunk and a scraping, as the dinghy hit a rock on the other side. Panting with the effort, Hallie swung the oar over and groped with it into the fog. The oar skidded across the rock on algae scum, and Hallie slipped off the seat, banged her knee on the boat bottom, and almost dropped the oar over the side. She cursed under her breath, got a better grip, and jabbed under the water again.

The oar was much heavier than it had seemed when it was fastened to the oarlock, and Hallie's arms were getting tired. She was sweating now, though only a few minutes before she had been cold. If only she could see! But the fog was even thicker, and the rocks rose out of the mist as suddenly as nightmares, too late to avoid them.

Thunk! Thunk! The boat jarred against another rock, or maybe it was one of those she'd already hit. Hallie hadn't cried, so far, except for those first few tears. She hadn't had time; she'd been working too hard, dragging the oars through the water. But now she heard herself whimper, a thin cry like the call of a gull.

She did care, she realized. She did want to be rescued. She didn't want to smash up against the rocks and fall into the icy water with no idea which way to swim. And, anyway, she couldn't swim well enough to stay afloat for long in the icy, autumn ocean. Oh, why hadn't she stayed on the beach? Too late now, she thought grimly, and then bit her tongue as the boat struck another rock so hard that one side dipped briefly under the waves and cold seawater washed over Hallie's legs. Although she knew that nobody would hear her, she cried out, "Help!"

SWIM BACKWARD.

The voice seemed to come from all around Hallie, as if the fog itself had spoken. Or it spoke inside her mind, so that she hadn't heard it so much as felt it, reverberating in her bones and muscles like her own heartbeat. Hallie froze, kneeling on the dinghy floor in a puddle of seawater, listening. But all she heard now were foghorns and gulls and the lapping of waves against her boat. Had she heard the voice or had she imagined it?

Imagination, it must have been, she decided. Either that or she was going crazy. But just as she began to probe again under the water with her oar, the voice spoke again.

SWIM YOUR SHELL BACKWARD, THE WAY YOU CAME, it said, silently, loudly, all around Hallie and inside her and nowhere at all. The voice was oddly musical, rising and falling almost the way the foghorns did, but not so sad and lonely. It was a kind voice, but beginning to sound a little impatient.

GO BACKWARD. THERE ARE NO ROCKS BEHIND YOU.

Of course there aren't, thought Hallie. How stupid I am. First there were no rocks, then there were rocks, and I've been drifting ahead all this time, so behind me must be the cove, and safe water. Imagination, craziness, whatever it was, the voice made sense.

For a moment Hallie was too busy organizing her oars and reattaching the loose one in the oarlock to question what she'd heard. She dipped the oars in the water and then she stopped. How did you row a boat backward, anyway? Hallie had no idea. She couldn't even make it go forward. Maybe if she turned around in the seat, so that she was facing the other way, it would be easier.

Hallie stood up in the boat and stepped over the seat, balancing herself against the dinghy's rocking. She turned around, but before she could sit down, the dinghy thunked once more against a sunken rock, jarring so hard this time that one side lifted right out of the water and Hallie lost her balance.

She saw the gray water rising up to meet her as she fell, and she had time to think, almost calmly, that she wished she were a better swimmer. Then she felt the first shock of ice as the water hit her skin, so cold it drove the air out of her lungs in a grunt, and she felt it pulling her down, deep and cold and unforgiving. Somebody help me, thought Hallie hopelessly, and then the water closed over her head.

Cold, cold, cold, so cold that in the first shocked plunge all thoughts left Hallie's mind. She opened her eyes and saw murky greenness, opened her mouth and it filled with brine. She flailed frantically against the water with wet, heavy arms and legs, but she wasn't sure which way was up. She closed her eyes again and felt darkness begin to flood her chest, but then the voice spoke again.

TRUST THE WATER, it said, from all around her, deeper and stronger, more reverberating than before.

STOP FIGHTING. TRUST. THE WATER WILL LIFT YOU.

Hallie was too cold, too frightened to wonder what was speaking to her, but she knew, dimly, that trusting this deep, dreadful iciness all around her was beyond her strength. She struggled against the water again and managed once to force her face up through the waves for one brief gasp of sweet air. But she was too weak and her wet clothes too heavy, and she slipped back down under the sea into the green, formless world of no up and down.

At once, the voice was all around her again. *TRUST ME, THEN,* it said. *I WILL LIFT YOU.*

She could not trust the water, but trusting the voice was easy. Too exhausted to try to understand, Hallie stopped fighting the huge, green, freezing sea and did as the voice told her. She let go, stopped her ineffective kicking and splashing, and that was when she felt the lifting—not in her body, but more like something under her soul. A deep, sure strength propelled her upward, made her strong enough so that this time, when her face broke through the waves again, she could kick strongly and stroke with her arms to keep herself there, while she filled her lungs with one shuddering breath, then another, then one more of sweet, salty, damp sea air. The lifting held her there, a sure, warm pressure from below so strong that she rested on it, lost her fear, forgot how cold she was, and opened her eyes, sputtering and sneezing as she shook the seawater away.

Just in front of her, a large rock, slimy with green algae, rose out of the mist like a friend. She reached out and grabbed it, dragged her wet body to the rock and clung, pulling more gasps of air into her lungs.

The voice didn't speak now, but Hallie could still feel its presence, holding her steady against the rock as if the water itself had changed from her enemy to her friend. She was still waist-deep in the ocean, and she knew, dimly, that the September air should have sliced freezing through her wet clothes, but she felt no cold. Somehow the presence that had lifted her was keeping her warm.

NOW MORE, the voice directed. Obediently, Hallie pulled herself higher onto the rock, dragging her body up over the slick, wet surface. The mist was beginning to thin, and now Hallie could see more rocks, blue mussel shells, tangles of seaweed. The rock she clung to wasn't an island, alone in the cove; it was part of the shore. She recognized a massive gray boulder jutting out into the sea beyond the rock she was clinging to, half-submerged in the foamy waves like a sleeping whale. It was Whale-back Rock, at the very end of the point, where the cove met the open ocean. She was ashore.

The knowledge gave her a surge of strength of her own, and she pulled herself farther out of the icy ocean. As she dragged herself up, she heard the voice once more.

GOOD, SMALL ONE. NOW HOLD YOURSELF.

And then, as Hallie drew her feet out of the icy water, the voice was gone, as suddenly as if she had never heard it at all. With the voice went the sense of strength and lifting, and as that left her, Hallie was suddenly small and alone and aware that she was dreadfully cold.

She huddled against the gray wall of Whaleback a moment, hugging herself with her wet arms, too bruised and exhausted to move. But the damp air bit through her soaked clothes as though she were naked, and her teeth chattered violently. Although the voice was gone now, some memory of its strength forced her out of her huddle and up onto her own shaky legs.

She stood, leaning against Whaleback Rock. Through what was left of the fog, she could see the sumacs and wild roses on the point, and beyond them, the pebbled causeway that led alongside the cove, back to the sandy shore and the steps that led up the bluff toward home. She drew in a shuddering, grateful breath of the cool morning air, and glanced back at the silent water.

"Thank you," Hallie said through her shivering to the green water that had somehow let her go, lapping quietly now against the rocks as if it were nothing more than the ordinary ocean she had seen every day of her life. "Whatever you are, whoever you are, thank you for helping me."

Then, hugging herself, she turned away from the water and began to run, shivering with cold, staggering unsteadily on the uneven rocks, toward home and warmth and dry clothes.

2

The kitchen was quiet and blessedly warm. Shivering, Hallie eased the porch door shut behind her. Her father's blue coffee mug with the whales on it stood untouched on the shelf. That meant he hadn't come downstairs yet. Maybe, if Hallie was lucky, he was still asleep and hadn't noticed that she had been gone.

Her mother's crooked clay mug that Hallie had made in the third grade stood beside Josh's plastic cup with the frog in the bottom. Neither had been touched since Monday, Labor Day, when Josh got burned. He had been in the hospital ever since. Her mother had stayed with him the whole time, and for most of that time, her father had, too. But Hallie had not been to the hospital at all.

It was Friday now. At first, Hallie had stayed with her Aunt Rose, who lived near the hospital in Portland. Aunt Rose had driven her to the middle school in the city for the first two days of the new school year. Hallie and her father had come home Thursday night, but Hallie's mother wouldn't leave Josh's side, and nobody knew when Josh might be able to come home.

Hallie glanced up at the kitchen clock. 6:30. Only a little over an hour had passed since she had slid out of her window in the gray light of dawn to sneak down to the beach. It seemed much longer than that. Now, with luck, she could get into the shower before her father caught her soaking wet. He had enough on his mind, worrying about Josh. And how could Hallie explain what had happened? She didn't understand it herself.

The shower was in the only bathroom in the house, on the first floor. Like most Garnet Island houses, the Rainsfords' house had originally been built as a summer cottage. It was full of old-fashioned Victorian charm— lacy wooden gingerbread on the shady front porch, narrow pine wainscoting on the inside walls, window seats overlooking the harbor and the city beyond. But the house was built so flimsily that from upstairs in her bedroom, Hallie could hear every word anyone said downstairs. That was why she couldn't cry in her own room—her father would have heard her right away. It had been hard enough to work the stiff, old window by her bed open without a squeak, so that she could get outside that morning. Everything in the house creaked, and sometimes, in high winds, the whole house rocked like a ship at sea.

The living room floorboards squeaked loudly under Hallie's feet as she started for the bathroom, and right away her father's voice floated down the stairs. "Hallie? Is that you down there?"

"Hi, Dad. I'm just taking a shower," Hallie called back, hoping her voice sounded normal. She ducked past her mother's piano into the bathroom as her father thumped down the narrow stairs. Hallie closed the bathroom door behind her just in time, as he stepped into the living room.

"Your mom called a few minutes ago. She wanted to talk to you before you went to school, but you weren't in your room," he said through the closed door. "Where did you go so early?"

Hallie was stripping off her wet clothes, shuddering as the cool bathroom air struck her damp, salty skin. "Um . . . just down to the beach for a walk, Dad," she said. She didn't think her shivering made her voice shake too much. Maybe her father wouldn't notice.

"Ah, you met Melissa for one of your before-school confabulations. Another meeting of the naiads," her father said. It wasn't a question. He had always loved to tease Hallie and Melissa by calling them the naiads, because, he said, they made him think of Greek mythological water spirits, wandering by the sea with dreamy looks on their faces.

Until lately, Hallie had always enjoyed her father's gentle teasing. But today she could tell he was only poking fun out of habit. His deep voice, even through the door, had that new, vague, almost bewildered sound it had had since Josh got hurt, as if he wasn't thinking about what he was saying.

Hallie turned on the shower spray and let its rushing noise answer her father. She would just let him believe that she had met Melissa. It was much easier than trying to explain what had really happened.

"Your mom said Josh had a better night," her father said through the door. "He managed to sleep a little."

27

"Good." Hallie stared at the blank, closed door. She thought she might freeze to death if she couldn't get into the warm shower soon. And why was it a *good* night if Josh had only slept a little? What were the rest of his nights like?

Nobody had told Hallie very much about Josh's injuries. All her father had said was that he wasn't as badly hurt as they'd feared at first. Only one of his legs was burned, and the doctors thought it would heal quickly. But if that were true, thought Hallie, why did her father seem so lost and worried? Why couldn't Josh come home? Why couldn't Hallie visit him, at least?

"I wish I could see him, Dad," she said to the closed door.

"No, no, your mother's right," her father answered. "You know about the hospital rule."

Hallie sighed sharply. She hadn't seen Josh since the day of his accident. It was bad enough that her mother wouldn't let her visit. But why did her father have to agree with her? Her mother said that the hospital didn't allow visitors under twelve. But Hallie would be twelve in only a few months, and she wanted to see her brother so badly that it hurt.

"Better make that shower quick, sweetheart," her father said. "You only have a few minutes to catch the boat to school."

"I know, Dad," said Hallie through chattering teeth. The floor creaked as her father walked away, and at last there was silence from the other side of the bathroom door. Hallie could picture her father, his big shoulders hunched in that new, tense way, wandering away across the dining room the way he did these days, as if he were lost in his own house.

The bathroom was filling with steam, deliciously warm against Hallie's clammy nakedness. She pushed back the shower curtain and stepped under the spray. The water was so much warmer than her cold skin that at first it burned like fire. She stood shuddering under the spray until its heat gradually warmed her muscles and the shivering passed.

The water drummed on her head and on the steel sides of the shower stall. As she always did in the shower, Hallie reached out and banged gently on the shower stall side. The metal reverberated like thunder. The banging was a bathroom ritual that should have been comforting, but today, Hallie wished she hadn't done it.

The sound made her think of Josh, who loved to make bathroom thunder, banging and banging on the shower stall, laughing with glee, until the shampoo bottles balanced on the narrow top fell off and their father yelled at him to stop. Hallie squeezed her eyes shut under the shower spray and willed the memory away. Even though he wasn't home, Josh was all over the house.

As she pushed away the thought of Josh, others crept in. Against the screen of her closed eyelids, as the water fell around her, Hallie suddenly saw freezing green seawater and felt herself sinking. She opened her eyes and scrubbed shampoo furiously into her scalp, but the image refused to go away.

She had almost drowned. What had saved her? Had she really heard that strange voice, or had she had some kind of hallucination because she had been so close to drowning? It hadn't seemed like a hallucination. The voice had sounded at least as real as anything in the ordinary world. Just remembering it as she stood under the warm shower, Hallie felt again something of the comfort, the sense of support and flowing, spreading joy that had driven away the fear and cold of the ocean. Whose voice had it been? Would whoever it was speak to her again?

"Hello? Whatever you are—whoever helped me—are you still there?" Hallie spoke out loud. She stood still and listened, but heard nothing but the drumming of the shower against the metal stall. Feeling stupid, she shook herself, turned off the faucet with an angry twist, and climbed out of the shower. She dried herself fiercely, trying to scrub away her thoughts—of Mr. Gianopoulos's dinghy, empty and drifting out to sea on the ebbing tide, of the voice, of Josh.

She wrapped her towel around herself and blinked dubiously down at her clothes in a damp pile on the bathroom floor. Long strands of slimy green seaweed were plastered on her shorts, and her T-shirt was smeared with green scum. How was she going to explain these to her father? There wasn't time to sneak them into the washing machine before school, and, anyway, the machine was in the kitchen, right under her father's nose.

Moving quickly, Hallie opened the bathroom window, scooped up her clothes, and dropped them neatly out the window into the space between the house wall and the lilac bush. There they lay, screened from sight by the wide green leaves. She could get them later and wash them when her father wasn't home.

Past the lilac leaves, Hallie could see the bay, spangled with morning sun now that the fog had lifted. Across the harbor lay the city, its waterfront a forest of masts among the docks, its old brick buildings softly rose-colored in the morning light. Jutting up among them like uneasy guests were the new concrete skyscrapers of the banks and hotels, and, on top of the hill, largest of all, Maine General Hospital, where Josh was. Hard sparks of white light reflected off its banks of windows, hurting Hallie's eyes. The building glared, huge and forbidding, no place for a little boy.

Hallie blinked and looked away. Then across the harbor floated the long blare of a horn. Hallie knew that sound as well as she knew her father's voice. It was the warning blast of the 7:15 ferry as it left the dock in the city, and it meant Hallie had exactly seventeen minutes until the boat docked at the island and she had to climb aboard or be late for school. She slammed the window shut and ran out of the bathroom and up the stairs, clutching her towel around her.

Hallie had had years of practice in getting dressed fast, and in only a few minutes she was back in the kitchen in her jeans and yellow sweatshirt, yanking a comb through the damp tangles of her long, brown hair. The phone had rung while she was dressing, and her father was talking to someone. He was using his professor voice, sounding the way he used to before Josh got hurt—crisp, competent, and authoritative. Busy trying to pry a bagel out of the toaster without burning her fingers, Hallie only half heard what he was saying.

"What kind of whales?" He listened for a moment. "Hmm. That's unusual. Well, I'm on my way in now. We can discuss it when I get there." He hung up the phone and turned to Hallie, and as he did, his shoulders hunched again and that vague, confused look settled back over his face like a mask.

"That was my lab assistant. Says there's been some kind of whale sighting in the harbor."

"Mmm." Hallie wasn't paying attention. She was spreading cream cheese on her bagel and thinking about her route to the ferry. The best way to get to the boat—especially when she was late—was the shortcut, a footpath that led from Hallie's yard through a patch of woods, past Melissa's house, and behind the day-care center playground to come out just up the hill from the ferry landing.

But if she went that way today, she'd probably meet Melissa, and something about what had happened to Hallie that morning made her reluctant to do that. She felt guilty about Mr. Gianopoulos's dinghy, floating abandoned out to sea. She ought to tell Melissa about it, so her father could go get it back. But if she did, she'd have to tell her how she knew where it was. She'd have to tell Melissa that she had taken the dinghy out on the cove.

And then she'd have to tell Melissa about falling into the water, and about the voice she'd heard. Hallie had always told Melissa everything. But she wasn't ready to talk about this yet, even to Melissa. She wanted to keep the voice to herself a little longer, to give herself a little time to think about it.

No, it would be easier not to see Melissa just yet. If she wanted to be sure not to run into her, she'd have to go the long way around, by Ocean Avenue. Hallie glanced up at the clock. 7:10. She would have to run all the way.

Hallie stood up and slung her backpack over her shoulder. "Got to run, Dad," she said through a mouthful of bagel.

Her father was frowning at the kitchen floor. "Hallie, there seem to be puddles on this floor," he said. "And is that seaweed?"

"Oh!" Hallie saw in dismay that she had left a slimy trail of damp footprints across the kitchen. She backed toward the door, clutching her bagel. "Um . . . I was wading, Dad. Sorry."

Her father blinked at her. "Isn't it a little cold for wading?"

But Hallie was at the door by then. "I'll mop the floor when I get home, okay?" she promised. "Have to go now, or I'll miss the boat." She let the screen door fall closed between them.

"Why not ride down in the Jeep with me?" her father asked through the screen.

"That's okay," Hallie called over her shoulder as she fled across the porch. "I need the exercise. See you on the boat!"

"Okay, then. See you." Hallie's father's voice floated absently through the screen. She ran down the walk in relief. Her mother would never have let her get away with that lame excuse about wading. Hallie wouldn't wade in the icy September ocean, and her mother would have known it. But her father was so preoccupied these days that he would believe anything Hallie told him. And that was good, Hallie thought as she ran past her mother's blue asters scattered like a cloud of stars along the walk, because there was no way she could have told him the truth about the events of that morning.

The road was a packed dirt lane, rutted and potholed from years of neglect. Hallie's family liked it that way. The potholes meant that tourists chose other island roads to explore in their big, noisy mainland cars, and bored island teenagers went elsewhere for their drag races. Hardly anyone drove on the road except for the handful of families who lived there, and most of them came to the island only in the summers. The Rainsfords' road had so little traffic that Josh and his friends could safely play a whole kickball game right in the middle of it. In exchange for the safety and quiet, the Rainsfords put up with the dust on their curtains and the damage to the springs of the Jeep without complaint.

Hallie's feet kicked up puffs of dust as she loped easily past pretty wooden cottages, stands of birch and pine trees, and tangles of wild roses and bittersweet. Running for the ferry never made her breathless. A lifetime on Garnet Island, where there was always a ferry to catch and never quite enough time to catch it, had given her, like most islanders, the stamina of a cross-country runner.

She snatched a few bites of her bagel as she ran, listening for the telltale sound of the ferry engines to time her progress. She couldn't see the ferry through the trees, but its steady throb rose above the soft pounding of her feet, the distant roar of the surf and the cries of the gulls, telling her that the boat was docked and waiting, and that she didn't have much time.

Missing the boat would be a disaster. The next ferry didn't come to the island for an hour, and if Hallie had to take that one, she would miss the school bus waiting at the city pier, have to pay a taxi to get across the city to school, and be more than an hour late to her classes.

She ran faster as she rounded the curve where the dirt road met the paved sweep of Ocean Avenue, the main road that wound all the way around the island's four-mile circumference. Now she could see other stragglers emerging from lanes and footpaths from all directions, hurrying down to the landing—carpenters lugging toolboxes, young women in business suits and running shoes, high school students in athletic jackets trying to look cool and unconcerned as they ran, mothers trotting behind strollers in which babies joggled as the wheels jounced over ruts.

There was no sign of Melissa. Hallie tried to ignore the little stab of loneliness that shot through her at the thought of her friend. It felt strange to run for the boat without her. For all their elementary school years, as they walked back and forth from the small island school, Hallie and Melissa had talked about how great things would be when they got to the sixth grade. Then they would be among the "big kids" who rode the ferry to the city every morning to Harborside Middle School. They had daydreamed about what it would be like—stopping for a doughnut at the island market before climbing on the boat; talking on the ferry all the way to Portland; sticking together as they faced the new kids at the city school, so big and exciting and different from the familiar island school where there were only thirteen kids in their whole grade.

Now that time was finally here, but it was nothing like Hallie had imagined. Everything she and Melissa had daydreamed about seemed unimportant in comparison to what had happened to Josh. She had seen very little of Melissa since the accident. Because she had been at her aunt's, she hadn't ridden the ferry to school at all. They had talked on the phone in the evenings, but she hadn't seen much of Melissa at school. They weren't in any of the same classes; they didn't even have lunch at the same time. By herself in the jostling, pushing crowds at the big city school, Hallie had felt alone and lost.

Hallie jogged past the grocery store and turned off Ocean Avenue onto the cobblestoned road that ran down the steep bluff to the landing, just as the boat, waiting at the dock, let out a peremptory toot, the one-minute warning. She could see the fat red and yellow ferry drawn up against the wooden pier below her. A stream of islanders was crossing the metal gangplank, while the deckhands loaded sacks of mail onto the boat and helped mothers with their strollers.

Her father's Jeep bounced past her on its wrecked suspension, one door tied shut with twine, and swung into the parking lot. Her father climbed out, newspaper clutched in one hand, coffee sloshing out of the mug in the other, and joined the river of islanders flowing down to the boat.

Hallie let her trot slow to a walk. She wouldn't miss the boat now; she was almost there. Mack, the captain, usually tried not to leave without people when he could see them running down the last stretch. But his courtesy meant that the 7:15 generally left the island a few minutes late, and every few weeks he would get exasperated and pull away from the pier even when latecomers were in sight, just to encourage everybody to get there on time.

As she stepped onto the silvered wooden planks of the pier, Hallie stopped and squinted over the glittering surface of the bay. From here, she couldn't see Whaleback Rock, on the ocean side of the island where she had pulled herself out that morning. This bright, glittering sea under a friendly blue sky was nothing like the cold, gray, hungry ocean that had pulled her down in the morning mist. It was impossible to believe she had been in that water, more impossible to believe that some strange voice had spoken to her through those bright waves breaking into foam on the rocks. If not for the ache in her arm muscles and the traces of salt still stinging her blistered palms, Hallie would begin to think it had been a dream.

"Hey, Hallie, get on the boat already. We haven't got all day!" It was Ira, one of the deckhands, seventeen and broad shouldered, with a white flash of smile and bright blue eyes. Since last year, Hallie and Melissa had shared a crush on him, and until just a few days ago she would have been as devastated by the impatience in his voice as she was flattered that he knew her name. But today she just looked up, as startled as if she had been asleep and dreaming, and obediently followed the last stragglers across the gangplank onto the boat.

3

Behind Hallie, Ira and the other deckhand yanked loose the rough yellow hawsers, thicker than Hallie's arm, that roped the ferry to the pier. The engines churned as the boat gathered strength to pull away from the dock. Hallie's father stood nearby on the open deck among a group of other islanders. Hallie could hear them talking about Josh, asking her father if their family needed help. But to her relief, none of them paid any attention to her.

"Wait, wait!" A distant, frantic voice rose above the throb of engines. Hallie glanced over the boat railing, up the hill toward the grocery store. There, running hard around the corner was a small figure, long, black hair flying behind her. It was Melissa, waving as she pelted down the hill, shouting, "Wait for me!"

The deckhands were already pulling the heavy metal gangplank on board. They hadn't seen Melissa. Hallie ran over to Ira and tapped him on the shoulder.

"Ira, hold on," she said. "Here comes Melissa. Can you wait just a minute?"

Ira glanced up at Melissa's flying figure. She was halfway down the bluff. "We're awful late this morning. Mack'll be mad," he said, shaking his head. "But for you and Melissa, Hallie, hey, anything! Joe, hold on, we've got a runner."

Ira tossed the hawser back over a piling, and the two deckhands steadied the plank and waited as Melissa ran across the pier. Ira turned, concern suddenly clouding his suntanned face, and said, "Hallie, how's Josh, anyway?"

But Hallie was squeezing away through the crowds of islanders busy with morning chatter, looking for a place to hide. At the sight of Melissa, she had felt all over again that morning's new reluctance to talk to her oldest friend. But there was nowhere to hide on the ferry.

She paused at the top of the stairs that led down to the lower deck, where salt-spattered windows protected riders from the ocean breeze. Melissa might not look for her down there. Most of the other middle school kids rode together down there in a giggling gang, but Hallie had never liked the hot and stuffy lower deck. Except on the bitterest winter days, she preferred the open air on the upper deck, where she could see the busy harbor with its oil tankers and tugboats, and sailboats fluttering among the islands like butterflies among flowers.

But before she could duck down the stairs, a voice spoke behind her. It was Melissa, out of breath and laughing.

"Oh, that was close," she said. "I was sure I'd miss the boat that time. Good thing Ira likes me, or he wouldn't have waited, huh, Hallie?"

Hallie turned away from the stairs and smiled unwillingly. "I guess so," she agreed.

"Come on, let's go sit up front." Melissa turned and climbed the two steps that led to the small deck in the bow of the boat, in front of the pilothouse. Hallie followed her reluctantly. There was no way to do anything else without hurting her friend's feelings.

Melissa dropped with a sigh onto one of the two benches that fit into the pointed bow. It was the coldest and windiest spot on the boat, and this morning nobody else was there. The wind grabbed Melissa's shiny black hair and whipped it around her face. Hallie had always envied her friend's hair, so unlike her own unruly, light brown tangle. Melissa's family was Greek, though they had been in Maine for generations. Hallie's pale Irish skin either freckled or burned, but Melissa's was olive-gold, even in the dullest days of winter, and the bones of her wrists and ankles were as delicate and pretty as a bird's.

As the ferryboat chugged away from the island and set off across the bay toward the city, Hallie sat down on the other bench. She was trying to think of a way to explain why she hadn't met her friend that morning. But before she could come up with some explanation, Melissa spoke.

"Sorry I didn't meet you this morning. I bet you wondered where I was."

Hallie blinked in surprise. Before she could say anything, Melissa went on breathlessly.

"I was *so* late! I had to help Dad. His dinghy was gone from the beach, and he couldn't find it, and then he spotted it with the binoculars, drifting way out in the channel, almost over to Tourmaline Island. The tide took it out, I guess. Dad must not have tied it up tight yesterday, but he swears he did. He was furious! I had to go with him to borrow the Spinners' dinghy and help Dad load it on the truck, so he could take it out to get our dinghy back. Look, you can see him out there now."

Speechless, Hallie looked where Melissa was pointing. In the channel between Garnet and Tourmaline, a distant figure rowed patiently across the water toward a small, dark shape like a piece of floating driftwood. Even though he was too far off to see clearly, Hallie recognized Melissa's father's smooth, strong rowing strokes, and knew the floating speck for what it was—the dinghy she had lost in the cove.

She stared in dismay. She had been worrying in the back of her mind about the lost dinghy all morning. If it had drifted away, Mr. Gianopoulos would have had a hard time replacing it. The Gianopouloses couldn't afford much. Melissa's father was one of the last remaining Garnet Island lobstermen, still setting out onto the bay each day to check his traps in the *Thea*, the red and white lobster boat he had named after his wife.

There had once been many lobstermen on Garnet, but as the nearby city grew, the island had changed. Most islanders nowadays commuted to Portland for city jobs and city incomes, and property taxes on the island had soared. Lobsters were growing scarce, and many of the old-time lobstermen had turned to different work, or had moved to new anchorages far away from city congestion and city taxes. But the Gianopouloses loved Garnet Island and they had stayed, scraping along by selling lobsters to the wealthier island newcomers.

As Hallie watched anxiously, the small figure that was Mr. Gianopoulos drew close to the bobbing speck. "He's almost got it now," said Melissa. "That ought to cheer him up. Jeepers, Hallie, you could have heard him yelling this morning up at your house. Even Mom couldn't calm him down."

Hallie pulled her knees up onto the bench in front of her and hugged them, making herself into a tight, anxious ball. Both girls were quiet for a few minutes, watching the small rowing shape on the sea catch up with the dark spot that was the dinghy. Gulls wheeled over their heads, crying, and the bell buoy clanged in surprise as the ferry wake sent it rocking. The ferry chugged through a floating flock of brightly striped lobster buoys marking the spots where traps were set. Hallie looked automatically for the red and white stripes that marked Mr. Gianopoulos's buoys. There were two or three of them, dipping below the wake as the boat passed and then bobbing up again.

Melissa spoke again. "Hallie, I'm sorry. It was such a frantic morning, I forgot all about Josh. How is he?"

Hallie shrugged. "I don't know. Mom called this morning, but I didn't talk to her. I guess he doesn't sleep much."

"Your mom stayed over there again last night, huh?" asked Melissa.

Hallie nodded.

"My mother's going over to the hospital this morning," Melissa went on. Their mothers had been friends since Hallie and Melissa were babies. The two girls had been born the same week, and their mothers had pushed strollers around the island together and traded baby clothes. Now their mothers still saw each other every day and knew each other so well that sometimes their conversation sounded almost like code.

"She's worried about your mom," Melissa said. "She's going to bring her some clean clothes. I don't know if she can go in Josh's room, though. Can he have visitors yet?"

Hallie shrugged miserably. "I don't know. They won't let me visit at all. I'm too young."

"That's so stupid. Well, if they ever do let you see him, I'll go with you if you want." Melissa's small, round face was pinched and worried behind the strands of black hair blowing across it, and already a little hurt by Hallie's reticence.

Hallie put her face down onto her blue-jeaned knees and said nothing. After a moment, she felt the bench wobble as her friend moved over to sit down next to her.

"Hallie, what is it? I know you feel awful about Josh, but it seems like something else is wrong. Did you have a fight with your dad or something?"

Hallie pushed her face farther down into her jeans. She didn't answer. What could she say? The more she thought about the voice she had heard in the sea that morning, the more she thought she must be going crazy. And yet it hadn't felt crazy. It had felt the opposite of crazy—sane, joyful, perfectly right. But how could she explain the voice to Melissa? Whether she really was crazy or not, the story would sound as if she were.

Hallie could feel the waiting warmth of Melissa's quiet presence, but it wasn't comforting. A barrier seemed to divide her from her old friend. It would be easier if

Melissa would get mad and go away, she thought, but Melissa rarely got mad. Just this once, Hallie wished she would.

After a few moments, she felt her friend's small, warm hand on her shoulder. "Hallie? Don't you want to talk about it?"

Hallie tensed, about to shrug the hand away, but as she did, the loudspeaker on the pilothouse just above them crackled into life and Mack, the captain, spoke.

"Good morning, folks," he said. There was no r in *morning*, the way Mack said it. He had the strongest Down-East accent Hallie had ever heard. The summer people loved to hear Mack's tour patter over the loud-speaker as he took boatloads of tourists around the bay, showing them the sights. But Mack hardly ever used the loudspeaker to talk to the year-round islanders on the commuter boats. When he did, it meant something unusual was going on.

"You might have noticed we're a bit off our ordinary course this morning," he continued. "We're going to take a little side trip over by the shipyard. Might make us a few minutes later than we already are, but there's something in the harbor today I thought you'd like to see."

Melissa's hand left Hallie's shoulder, and the bench wobbled again as her friend stood up.

"We have some whales visiting the harbor this morning," Mack went on. "Watch to starboard, and you'll see their spouts. Look sharp as we get closer. You'll see their backs as they come up to breathe."

"Whales!" Melissa's voice was excited. There were

seals in the harbor sometimes, but never whales. The harbor was too shallow, too polluted, too full of the comings and goings of human beings.

"Hallie, I'm going to see them. Come on!" Melissa's footsteps pattered away, but Hallie didn't move. She was tired of whales. They were her father's specialty, and all he ever talked about. And, anyway, why should she care about whales when her only brother was in the hospital and it was partly her fault, and now she was hearing voices and maybe going crazy, and couldn't even talk about it to her best friend?

The harbor breeze blew cold across the back of Hallie's neck, and she pulled her arms tighter around her knees. She had felt badly enough when Melissa was sitting beside her, but it was surprising how much worse she felt now that her friend's warm nearness had disappeared. This was the first time in her life that she had kept an important secret from Melissa. It was a lonely feeling. And then she thought, if I'm lonely here on this crowded, familiar boat, how does Josh feel in that big awful hospital? She couldn't imagine it. She swallowed down tears and mumbled into her knees, "I've never felt so alone in my life."

ALONE? WHAT DOES THAT MEAN?

The voice flooded into Hallie's mind just as it had before, from nowhere, from everywhere, part of the wind on her neck, part of the steady chug of the ferry engines throbbing into her bones, part of the regular beat of her own pulse.

Hallie sat up straight and looked around. "Hey! Who

are you? Where are you?" The benches around her were empty, and all she could see beyond the deck rail was the everyday waterfront, the shipyard with its tall cranes, the fishing boats unloading early catches onto the docks, the cars rushing along Waterfront Street. But as soon as she heard the voice, the mental picture of Josh that had been haunting her, white-faced, bandaged, crying in a hospital bed, disappeared. Suddenly, instead, Hallie remembered Josh before he got hurt, sitting up to his neck in the sunshiny ocean, laughing and sputtering as small waves slapped his freckled face. The memory made her smile, and the aching loneliness disappeared, replaced by an unreasonable, singing sense of joy.

I DO NOT KNOW ALONE. WHAT IS IT? The voice didn't use words, exactly. The sound in Hallie's mind was more like music, a wild, sweet, rushing sound something like the song of surf rolling and breaking on the rocks. But the music made sense, and Hallie understood its meaning as clearly as if the voice had spoken in English.

"Alone . . . well, it means all by yourself. Nobody else with you," Hallie tried to explain, though she didn't know to whom she was speaking. She spoke out loud, but there was nobody nearby to hear her. All the passengers had gone astern to see the whales. An indistinct hubbub of excited voices rose from the stern, but the pilothouse blocked Hallie's view.

ALONE. The voice tried out the idea, as if tasting it and finding it not to its liking. *HOW STRANGE.* Then it went on, as if giving up on something it couldn't quite understand. *YOU HAVE A NEW SHELL, NOW, SMALL ONE. THIS ONE IS LARGER, AND VERY NOISY.*

"A new shell ... oh, you mean the boat." Hallie grinned as she understood. "I lost the other one, when I fell out."

YOU WILL NOT FALL OUT OF THIS SHELL, TOO? The voice sounded troubled.

Hallie couldn't help giggling. The strange joy flooded through her like sunlight.

"I won't fall out," she promised. "That was an accident, before."

GOOD, said the voice. *YOU ARE SMALL, AND EASY TO HOLD. BUT IT IS HARD TO HOLD TWO AT THE SAME TIME.*

"To hold two ... I don't understand. Who are you, anyway?" Hallie stood up and looked over the deck rail, down at the surface of the harbor. This close to the city, the water was dirty, with scummy clumps of foam and bits of litter floating on the surface. Hallie was beginning to think that maybe the water itself was speaking to her. But it looked too sad and dirty and polluted to have any connection with the sweet, wild, pure sound of the voice.

I HELD YOU BEFORE, WHEN YOU LOST YOUR SHELL, the voice explained. *BECAUSE YOU ARE JUST A CALF, AND NOT A SWIMMER. BUT I CANNOT HOLD YOU AND GLOBO, TOO.*

"Globo?" repeated Hallie. Instead of saying the name, the voice had made a complicated, whistling sound, but with the whistling, the word *Globo* had spoken itself in

Hallie's mind. With the name came an odd feeling, a bittersweet sense of tenderness and concern.

GLOBO, whistled the voice again. *I AM HOLDING HIM WHILE HE IS HEALING.*

The loudspeaker over Hallie's head crackled again. "We're getting closer to the whales now," Mack's voice announced. "Professor Rainsford, here, tells me they're pilot whales, also known as potheads. Look close when they come up to breathe, and you may be able to see the bulge on their foreheads that gives them the nickname. The professor says that at least one of them seems to be sick or injured." The boat engines throbbed as Mack brought the ferry around.

The voice broke through Mack's announcement in Hallie's mind. *SWIM YOUR SHELL AWAY, PLEASE, SMALL ONE,* it said urgently. *YOU ARE TOO CLOSE. THE NOISE IS HURTING GLOBO.*

A sudden idea dawned in Hallie's mind. "Are you . . . are you a whale?" she asked the voice in excitement. "Is Globo a whale, too?"

I DO NOT KNOW THIS WHALE, answered the voice impatiently. *BUT THIS NOISE HURTS GLOBO. SWIM YOUR SHELL AWAY, QUICKLY.*

Hallie bit her lip. "I can't steer the boat," she said anxiously. "I'm not the captain."

But the sound of the voice in her head was changing, the joy ebbing out of it. *TOO MUCH NOISE,* it said, sounding frightened. *I CANNOT HOLD GLOBO MUCH LONGER.*

The loudspeaker crackled again, and Mack spoke. "We're running very late today, folks, and we'll have to head into port now. But I hope you've enjoyed our visitors."

The ferryboat swung away from the shipyard and the engines picked up speed as the ferry headed past the fishing docks toward the landing.

"Hello? Are you still there? Are you all right?" asked Hallie anxiously.

For a moment, no answer came, but then the voice spoke again, sounding a little calmer. *THAT IS BETTER. THANK YOU, SMALL ONE.* The lilting music and sense of joy was coming back, and Hallie's heart lifted in response.

Hallie leaned over the rail and craned her neck, trying to spot the whales past the pilothouse and the crowd of passengers still thronging the stern. Far behind the boat, close to the water, she caught a fleeting glimpse of a puff of steam like a small cloud. Something slippery and black gleamed briefly just above the waves and then vanished again.

"That *is* you, isn't it," Hallie cried. "You're one of the whales. And Globo is the other whale, and he's too sick to swim by himself. You're helping him, the same way you helped me this morning, when I was drowning."

YOU MAY CALL US WHALES IF YOU LIKE, SMALL ONE, said the voice.

Hallie stared in wonder at the glittering bay, disappearing now beyond the end of the pier as the ferryboat drew up alongside the landing ramp. The other passengers were picking up their newspapers and briefcases, getting ready to get off the boat as if nothing unusual had happened. She could hear the deckhands yelling to each other as always, and the loud metallic screeching of the gangplank as they dragged it into position for the passengers to disembark.

Nobody else seemed to have heard the whale. Could it really be true that she had heard it? Why Hallie, and nobody else? But it seemed to be true. And it didn't feel strange. It felt like the simplest, most natural thing in the world.

As the passengers streamed across the gangplank and headed past the ticket office and the newspaper machines and the fish market toward the bustle of downtown, Hallie stood still on the ferryboat, holding on to the rail. "You told me that the other whale's name is Globo," she said. "But who are you? Do you have a name?"

The voice made another sound like musical whistles, rising and falling in Hallie's mind like a complicated bird song. A name spoke itself in her mind, and with the name came again that deep sense of joy and comfort. "Melae," repeated Hallie gladly. "Your name is Melae."

MELAE, whistled the voice in agreement, but as it did, something tapped Hallie on the shoulder, and another voice, an ordinary human one, spoke in Hallie's ear.

"Hey, Hallie, what are you waiting for? You're day-dreaming again. You're the last one on the boat!" It was Ira, the deckhand, coiling a rope under the bench as he spoke.

Hallie looked around, blinking. It was true. There was nobody left on the ferry but Hallie and the deckhands. On the dock, she could see Melissa and her father among the crowd of islanders walking toward the street, where the school bus was waiting. As Hallie watched, Melissa turned, squinted back at the ferry, and beckoned to Hallie impatiently.

"Oh . . . thanks, Ira." Hallie picked up her backpack, jumped down the steps and ran across the deck to the gangplank.

"Hello, Melae," she said to the voice as she stepped onto the plank. "My name is Hallie."

But the whale did not answer. As Hallie trotted across the gangplank onto the landing, Melae's voice and that boundless sense of joy left her as suddenly and completely as it had when she had pulled herself out of the ocean. Hallie stopped short, shocked by the loneliness flooding through her. "Melae?" she said aloud. "Melae? Where did you go?"

But there was no response. The school bus driver honked the horn, and Melissa leaned out the bus door. "Hallie," she yelled. "Come on! We're already late!" Hallie shook herself, as if waking from a dream, and began to trot reluctantly up the pier. She looked back over her shoulder as she climbed up the bus steps. She could see the harbor beyond the end of the dock, sparkling in the sun, but she couldn't see the whales. Nothing spoke to her. All she could hear was the honking horns of the downtown traffic, and above them the lonesome crying of the gulls.

4

Hallie spent that day at school in a dream. She followed her schedule automatically from class to class, pushing her way through the hallways without seeing the jostling crowds. Her mind was full of the voice of the whale, her heart still high with the wonder and glory of it.

Everyone left her alone. In this first week of school, none of her teachers even knew her name. She had no classes with Melissa. Karen Alberts and Diane Pitcher, Garnet Island girls whom Hallie had known since kindergarten, were both in her English class. But as soon as Hallie walked in, they stopped talking abruptly, gave her quick, anxious smiles and then glanced away, as if they weren't sure where they ought to look. After their first shy hi's, they didn't talk to Hallie at all.

Hallie noticed, but without hurt, as if she were watching her old friends from a distance. A lot of her friends—almost everyone except Melissa, in fact—had been behaving strangely since Josh got hurt, as if they were afraid to talk to Hallie. She thought that maybe they were afraid that what had happened to her family was contagious; that the fire that had burned Josh might burn them, too, if they let themselves get too close. Or maybe they just didn't know what to say.

But today, with the memory of the whale's voice still singing joyfully in her mind, Hallie hardly noticed even when Karen passed a note to Diane, who read it and crumpled it up without a glance in Hallie's direction. Any other time, Diane would have handed it on to Hallie, and the three of them would have exchanged secret smiles. Hallie watched them calmly, seeing, instead of Diane's smile for Karen, the quick shining arc of wet, black whaleskin that had appeared above the surface of the bay and disappeared again before Hallie was sure of what she had seen. The teacher's voice droned in the hot classroom, and flies buzzed against the closed windows, but Hallie heard only the singing rhythm of her memory of Melae's voice.

But still she couldn't hear the whale herself. All day she listened, but she heard nothing except the ordinary human voices of the teachers and students around her. At lunch, Hallie took her sandwich outside, to a grassy bank topped with a grove of willow trees that divided the school from a neighboring complex of office buildings. Technically, middle school students weren't allowed out there, but it wasn't hard to slip out of the crowded cafeteria without being noticed by the harassed lunch monitor.

Hallie sat down in the sun-dried September grass, leaned her back against a willow trunk, and took a grateful breath of cool autumn air. Surely, out here in the quiet she would be able to speak to Melae again.

"Melae?" she whispered. "Melae, are you there?" She

closed her eyes and listened. Birds twittered in the willow branches, distant cars hummed past, and a giggle floated, now and then, out of the tangled bushes under the willows where the high school girls went with their boyfriends.

But that was all she heard. No voice spoke, no singing whistles echoed through her mind. The laughter in the bushes grew louder, and a gang of boys from the high school wrestling team came yelling up the bank and started practicing holds on each other in the grass. Still, the haze of happiness stayed in Hallie's heart. She pressed her back into the rough bark of the willow tree and thought how strange it was that she had gotten along perfectly well until today without talking to a whale, but now she felt as if nothing mattered in the world but speaking to the whale again.

When the school day ended at last, Hallie let herself be carried out the front door, tossed along in a flood of students eager to escape the stuffy classrooms for the bright September afternoon. Hallie didn't notice the crowds around her. She was remembering the way Melae had called boats shells. It made sense if you were a whale. She smiled to herself as she followed Diane and Karen toward the bus that carried the island students across the city to the boat landing.

But as Hallie put one foot onto the bus step, Melissa came up behind her and poked her in the ribs.

"Hey, Hallie, there's your mother. She's calling you."

Startled, Hallie looked up. In the school parking lot, beyond the line of yellow buses, her mother stood beside their car, waving at her frantically.

Hallie felt her smile fall off her face as if she had dropped it. Her mother had hardly left Josh's room since the day he got hurt. Why was she here now? Maybe Josh was worse.

"Well, go on," urged Melissa. "You better see what she wants."

But Hallie stood still by the bus for another moment, her heart like a stone in her chest. Josh. For the first time since he got hurt, she had forgotten all about him. Her mind had been so full of the whale and the wonder of what had happened in the early morning that she had hardly thought of her brother all day. Now, memory fell back over Hallie like a dark cloak, and with it, guilt. How could she have forgotten him for so long?

When Hallie finally pushed her way through the crowds and past the buses, her mother met her with a tired smile. "Oh, Hallie, I've missed you," she said, and held out her arms.

Stiff and reluctant at first, Hallie let her mother embrace her. It had been a long time since they had hugged. During the last year, Hallie had grown taller than her mother, and since that happened she had thought of herself as too old for hugs. Lately, too, she and her mother had been arguing a lot.

But she had forgotten how warm her mother's arms were, and forgotten, too, the spicy smell of her curly red hair and the smoothness of her freckled skin. Hallie's arms seemed to come up by themselves to hug her, and she let her head drop onto her mother's soft, cotton shoulder. She forgot that she ought to be embarrassed, hugging her mother in front of the entire assembled student body of the Harborside Middle School. She forgot that she had forgotten Josh. She even forgot the whale.

It was the roar of the school buses, lumbering away from the curb like yellow dinosaurs, that reminded her. Hallie picked up her head and stepped out of the circle of her mother's arms. "Mom, why are you here?" she asked. "Is Josh worse?"

"Oh, no, honey." Now Hallie noticed how tired her mother looked, her eyes shadowed with fatigue, new lines cutting sharply from her nose to the corners of her mouth. Her hair had never been neat, but today the coppery curls were wilder than ever, as if it had been a long time since her mother had even tried to get a comb through them. "No, he isn't worse. He's a little better, actually. They moved him from the burn unit to pediatrics today. Your dad's with him right now. He was asleep when I left."

"Why did you come?" Hallie asked again. "I was afraid something bad had happened."

"No, sweetie." Her mother patted her shoulder. "Nothing new. Your dad insisted that I get away from the hospital for a while, and I wanted to see you. I picked up some groceries for you and Dad to take home on the ferry, and I thought you could ride up with me to the hospital first to see Josh."

"See Josh! Are you going to let me visit him after all?" Hallie stopped in the act of climbing into the car.

"Oh, no." Her mother climbed into the driver's seat as Hallie got into the other front seat. "I just meant you can wave to him from outside. He can look out his window. The hospital doesn't allow visitors under twelve, Hallie."

"But, Mom, I'll be twelve in December."

"I know, but the rule is the rule."

"The rule is stupid," said Hallie. "I'm not poisonous, you know, just because I'm under twelve."

"No, but children do carry a lot of germs, and burns can easily get infected."

"I'll have just as many germs when I'm twelve as I do now. Mom, I really want to see him," pleaded Hallie.

"The best thing you can do for Josh right now is to let him rest, so he can get better. There's really nothing else you can do. I know you miss him, but it's settled, sweetie." Her mother set her lips in a firm line. Hallie knew from experience that there was no point in arguing with her mother when her mouth looked like that.

As her mother turned the key, the car leaped easily to life. Like most island families, the Rainsfords had a mainland car and an island car. The Jeep was their island car, old and rusty, but good enough for quick jaunts to the ferry or the grocery store. It often wouldn't start without several tries and maybe a slap or two on the dashboard; sometimes it wouldn't start at all. The mainland car was newer and cleaner, and it never had to be slapped. All the same, Hallie liked the Jeep better. With its door tied shut with string, and sand all over the seats, it felt more like home.

Hallie watched the city move past the car windows—brick apartment buildings, the white towers of the university where her father taught, banks and gas stations and furniture stores. The lump was still in her throat. Maybe her mother was right. Maybe Josh was so badly hurt that it was better for her to stay away. But how bad was that? It had to be so terrible Hallie could hardly imagine it. When Josh had had the flu the year before, Hallie had practically moved into his room with him, reading him stories and playing endless games of checkers. Obviously, this was different.

Hallie stole a quick sideways look at her mother's profile, absorbed in her driving as she maneuvered through the city traffic. Hallie had had almost no opportunity to talk to either of her parents about the accident since Josh got hurt. She had hardly seen her mother at all. It was hard to talk to her father even at ordinary times, and since Josh's accident, he had been even more preoccupied than usual, so worried about Josh and lonely without Hallie's mother that Hallie didn't want to trouble him.

She looked quickly away, at the last autumn roses blooming in the city garden at the edge of the park. The roses blurred before her eyes into a smear of pink and cream.

"Mom," she said finally, forcing the question past the lump in her throat. "Are you sure Josh is getting better?"

"Of course he is," said her mother swiftly. Maybe a little too swiftly. Was she telling the truth, or covering it up to try to comfort Hallie? Her mother was always trying to protect her, treating her like a little girl. I'm too old to believe in Santa Claus, you know, Mom, Hallie wanted to say. But she kept quiet.

"Kids heal quickly, you know," her mother went on. "The doctors seem to think he's doing very well."

Something in the way her mother's voice trailed off at the end of the sentence made Hallie ask, "But, Mom, what do *you* think?"

"Oh, I don't know." Her mother's answer came suddenly, in a sad, bewildered rush, as if she had forgotten for a moment that she was speaking to Hallie, not another grown-up. "He won't eat much. He doesn't sleep well. He seems . . . depressed or something."

"Is he going to die?" Hallie asked the question fast, before she could stop herself.

"No!" Her mother glanced at Hallie, her face shocked. "Of course not! It isn't that bad, Hallie. It's just that he's . . . well, he's sad. It was such a painful, scary thing. I don't think he knew such bad things could happen, before."

Though she could not have explained why, Hallie was suddenly furious, so angry that she could hardly see. She had forgotten the sweetness of their hug, forgotten how glad she had been, just a few minutes before, to be with her mother again. "So what are you doing about it?" she challenged.

Hallie's mother frowned at her, squinting a little, as if Hallie was shining a light into her eyes. "I stay with him all the time, Hallie. I read to him, and play games, and sing. And I . . . well, I pray a lot."

Hallie snorted. "Pray!" She didn't like the hateful tone of her own voice, but she couldn't seem to help it. "What good does that do?"

"A lot of good, I hope," said her mother gently.

"It won't," insisted Hallie. "Mom, it's a waste of time to pray. A god worth praying to wouldn't let something like this happen in the first place. If God could let a little boy like Josh get burned, why do you think He'll change His mind and help him now, just because you pray?" Her voice rose as she spoke so that by the time she finished, she was yelling, throwing words at her mother like stones.

"Hallie, just cut it out!" Her mother stomped hard on the brake as they came to a red light, so that Hallie jerked against the seat belt. She turned to glare at Hallie, the lines on her tired face harsh in the afternoon light. "Aren't things difficult enough, without you fighting with me on top of everything else? Don't you care about your brother at all?"

Hallie stared back at her mother. Oh, Mom, I do care, she was thinking. I care so much, and I can't do anything about it. You won't even let me see him. I care too much, Mom, can't you see? But it was useless to say any of this; her mother just wouldn't understand.

She turned away from her mother, folded her arms and scowled at the hospital looming ahead of them. As she watched, an ambulance howled through the gates, its red lights flashing, and rushed around the huge building toward the emergency entrance at the back. The light changed, and her mother swung the car into the hospital lot and parked in a space marked VISITORS. Neither of them spoke.

When the car stopped, Hallie flung open her door and scrambled away from her mother. Heat rolled up from the asphalt in waves and reflected off the windshields of the rows and rows of parked cars. Who did all these cars belong to, anyway, Hallie wondered. Were there so many people who had come to the hospital because somebody they loved was sick?

Her mother came up behind her and touched her arm. "I'm sorry, sweetie. Let's not fight. It's been a hard time for all of us. And I'm so tired, I guess it makes me grouchy."

"I'm sorry, too," mumbled Hallie, looking down at her feet. But she wasn't sure she was really sorry at all.

"Come on, Josh's window is this way," her mother said. Hallie followed her along the hospital wall, around the end of the building to a small patch of grass, planted around the edges with red geraniums, a little faded and tired now at summer's end. One lonely sapling stood in the center of the grass.

"His room's up there," said her mother, pointing. "On the second floor, the last window down at the end. See, the curtains are open. I'll go in and tell Josh you're here."

But before her mother moved, as Hallie squinted up at the anonymous square of glass in the long row of squares just like it, a tall, hunched shape appeared in the dimness behind the window. It was Hallie's father, his face and his white shirt pale blurs behind the glass. He waved, and Hallie and her mother waved back. Then her father moved away from the window.

Hallie could still see him dimly, doing something behind the glass. He was pushing the bed over to the window, she realized, and then the bed itself appeared, a large white blur like a rectangular cloud.

At first Hallie couldn't see Josh at all. But then something moved, a small shape like a starfish floating across the darkness about the white bed. It was a hand, Hallie realized slowly, waving to her. Uncertainly, she waved back. And then, once she had recognized his hand, she could follow the line of his arm and find the pale triangle of Josh's face under a darker blur of hair, distorted by the glass as if it were underwater. Hallie couldn't see his features through the glass, or the red of his curly hair, just the indistinct shapes, like a half-developed photograph. He looked smaller than she remembered, and very far away.

She took one small step forward. "Josh!" Her voice caught in her throat. The starfish hand waved again, weakly, and she could dimly see Josh's mouth moving, but she couldn't hear him through the glass. He looked so small up there, a tiny white blur in the dim greenish depths behind the window. Had he always been so small, or had he shrunk in the hospital?

"Tell Dad to open the window," she said to her mother. "I can't hear what Josh is saying."

"It doesn't open, honey. The hospital's air-conditioned. And, anyway, we can't be yelling up at windows at a hospital. We'd disturb people."

"But I want to talk to Josh!" protested Hallie. Above them, in the window, the starfish that was Josh's hand stopped waving and drifted back down onto the bed again. Hallie's father appeared again, pushing the bed away, so that Josh disappeared in the shadows beyond the glass.

"Wait!" Hallie cried. "What's Dad doing? I just got here!"

"Josh gets tired quickly," said her mother. "Your father probably thought that was enough excitement for now."

"I hardly saw him at all," Hallie objected halfheartedly. But all of a sudden, she felt too tired herself to argue about it. She was awfully tired, she realized suddenly, worn out, exhausted. She sat down abruptly on the grass in the scrap of shade cast by the one scrawny tree.

"I guess I'd better go up to Josh now." Her mother was still staring up at Josh's window, her shoulders drooping a little. "Your dad will be down to get you in a few minutes. The two of you are going to have to hurry, if you want to catch the ferry."

Her mother bent to give Hallie a quick, distracted kiss, as if she had already forgotten about her; as if, in her mind, she was already back inside the hospital, behind those blank, brick walls and the faceless windows that shut Hallie out. Then she was gone, her heels clicking as she hurried along the sidewalk toward the door.

Hallie closed her eyes. She was too tired to hurry to catch the ferry. She was too tired to think. She had been up, she remembered now, since before dawn. She had almost drowned, and there had been the whale speaking to her, and then she had swum through that cold water, and then there had been the boat ride, and the whale again, and then the long day at school, and then the fight with her mother, and the hospital, and Josh. Just remembering it all was exhausting. Hallie let her thoughts drop away from her, and by the time her father got there, she was almost asleep in the grass.

5

When her father shook her shoulder, Hallie roused herself reluctantly and stumbled after him to the car. He held the door for her as she dropped, yawning, into the passenger seat.

He got into the car and patted her shoulder awkwardly. "First week of school's got you tired out, I guess. And all this, too." His gesture took in the hospital behind them. Hallie just nodded and let her head drop back against the headrest.

"I think Josh enjoyed seeing you," her father said. There were shadows under his eyes, and the hair on top of his head stood straight up.

"I guess." Hallie was too tired to talk, and she was relieved when her father lapsed back into preoccupied silence as he drove down through the crowded streets of Lighthouse Hill, past gas stations, corner markets, weather-beaten wooden houses with rickety second-story porches hung with laundry. Children played on the sidewalks, darting dangerously close to the street as they passed.

At the boat landing, her father parked in their space in the parking garage. They lugged the sacks of groceries

Hallie's mother had bought down the steps, through the waiting room, and across the dock. Hallie's bag seemed unreasonably heavy. She was so tired that she hardly noticed Ira when he took her ticket as she crossed the gangplank. With a sigh of relief, she set down the bag and dropped onto one of the red-painted benches on the ferry deck.

Although the boat was crowded, no knot of sympathetic islanders gathered around Hallie and her father on this trip. On Fridays in September, summer people from the mainland came in droves to their island cottages for the weekend, so the deck was full of people Hallie didn't know. Her friends from school had all gone home on the earlier boat, while she had been at the hospital. Hallie was glad she wouldn't have to talk to anyone. She'd get up and look for Melae in a minute, she thought, but first, she wanted to rest a little. She leaned back against the hard slats of the bench and let her eyes fall shut.

The ferry sounded its long warning blast and chugged away from the dock. The familiar sounds and movement began to lull Hallie back into a comfortable half sleep. She jumped when, unexpectedly, her father's deep voice rumbled beside her.

"The Coast Guard must have managed to drive those whales out of the harbor," he said. "I don't see any sign of them out here tonight."

Hallie's eyes opened abruptly, and she sat up straight. "Drive the whales out? But why? Where did they go?"

"You don't have to yell in my ear, Hallie. I'm sitting right next to you," said her father grumpily.

"Sorry, Dad, I didn't mean to yell." Suddenly wide awake, Hallie jumped up and peered anxiously over the rail. The harbor spread out around the ferry, gleaming in the afternoon sun, the islands lying quiet in the water like sleeping green beasts. Over by the shipyard, where Hallie had caught that one brief, shining glimpse of black whaleskin that morning, nothing broke the surface. And in Hallie's mind, no voice spoke.

"But *why*, Dad?" Hallie turned desperately to her father. "Why would the Coast Guard drive them away? They weren't hurting anybody!"

"Well, I consulted by phone this morning with some whale specialists at the aquarium. They're sending a team up to investigate, but they felt somebody should try to drive the whales offshore into deeper water, right away. So I advised the Coast Guard, this morning, to try to get them out of the harbor."

"*You* told them to chase the whales away?" Hallie grabbed the rail behind her with both hands and hung on to it, hard. She was yelling again. "How could you do that, Daddy? They were beautiful!"

"Well, yes, of course they were," her father agreed. "You really must stop shouting, Hallie. We had to get the whales away from shore for their own good."

"Their own good! What are you talking about?" yelled Hallie. A tall woman next to her, in a sophisticated white outfit much fancier than anyone who actually lived on Garnet Island ever wore, turned to stare at Hallie, her eyebrows arched over the tops of her sunglasses. Hallie didn't care. She felt like sticking out her tongue at her.

"Hallie, please calm yourself. I do know something about this subject, you know. These were pilot whales, species *Globicephala melaena*, also called potheads or blackfish, although, as you know, they are not fish but mammals." Her father was getting that professorial look on his face, and Hallie realized in exasperation that she was in for one of his lectures. "In shallow water there is always the risk that pilot whales will strand themselves. By moving them into deeper water, where they belong, we're simply trying to make that less likely."

"Strand themselves? What does that mean?" demanded Hallie.

"Well, these whales sometimes swim onto beaches and get trapped." Her father was enjoying his explanation and didn't seem to notice Hallie's growing dismay. "It's especially likely when they are sick or injured. If one strands, others are likely to follow. Sometimes hundreds of them die this way."

"Well, *these* whales wouldn't have stranded themselves," insisted Hallie.

"How do you know?"

"I just know, that's all," cried Hallie furiously. "You shouldn't have told the Coast Guard to chase them away. What did they do, herd them with motorboats? It probably scared them, and hurt their ears! You shouldn't have told them to do that. It was dumb!"

The woman in sunglasses shook her head and turned her back. Hallie's father scowled.

"Now stop that at once, Hallie. You are being very unreasonable. This morning, you didn't even come and look at the whales. Your friend Melissa asked a number of intelligent questions, but you just sat in the bow daydreaming and ignored them. Why are you so interested now?"

Hallie stared dumbly at her father. She didn't want to believe that the whales were gone, but she could feel that it was true. The silence in her mind echoed like an empty room. Her father stared back at her, looking more confused than angry behind his glasses.

Finally, Hallie shook her head. "You don't understand, Dad," she said. "You don't understand at all."

Then she turned and pushed her way away from her father through the cheerful crowds of chattering weekenders, stepping over their suitcases, stumbling over their canvas bags loaded with bottles of wine and loaves of French bread, detouring around their carefully leashed dogs, till she found her way up to the windy bow of the boat, blessedly less crowded, and sat down heavily on the bench where she had spoken with Melae that morning.

"Melae?" she whispered experimentally. "Melae, are you there? Can you hear me?"

But no voice answered. Hallie stared bitterly across the water at Garnet Island as the ferry plowed toward it. The cottages lining the shore were as tiny and unreal at this distance as the toy houses that went with Josh's wooden train set.

Now I don't have anybody, she thought. Josh was locked away from her in the hospital. She had argued with both her parents that day. She had kept a secret from Melissa for the first time in their friendship.

And now even Melae was gone. When Hallie remembered how blissful she had felt all day at school, she couldn't believe how stupid she had been.

As the boat chugged closer to the island, Hallie listened gloomily to the ordinary noises of the harbor—the throb of the ferry engine, the calling of the gulls, the long blare of the horn on an oil tanker slowly steaming into the harbor—and behind all those everyday sounds, silence. No reverberating voice. No comforting, joyful presence.

The silence was as cold and lonely as it had been that morning, when the whale's voice had abruptly disappeared as Hallie got off the ferry, or when she had climbed out of the water at dawn. Both times, the whale's voice and that wonderful feeling of intimacy had vanished as suddenly as if a door had unexpectedly slammed shut between them. Why?

The boat had swung into its last curve, approaching the Garnet Island dock, when Hallie first heard the whistling. At first, she thought she was imagining it. Between the wind rushing in her ears and the chug of the engines under her feet, the bow was a noisy place. The sound she thought she heard, a strange, distant piping like a single flute, was faint and subtle, as if it might be part of the sound of the engines.

But the whistling grew steadily clearer and stronger, and gradually Hallie recognized that she was not imagining it, that she was hearing something real, something wonderful, something that took the sting out of her thoughts of her family and Melissa, and filled her with a deep, sweet comfort.

Around her, the other passengers in the bow read

their newspapers serenely, chatted with each other, took pictures of the harbor. Nobody else seemed to hear what Hallie heard.

But the music piped insistently through Hallie's veins, wild and wordless, a cascade of whistling like a jubilant flutist playing without a score. The harbor stretched around her, ordinary and empty; she could not see the whale. But as surely as she knew her own name, Hallie knew that what she heard was Melae, that the whale was swimming back to the harbor, and singing as she came.

Hallie grabbed the bench to keep herself from jumping up and down and yelling with joy. She contented herself with a wide, silly grin. "Melae," she whispered, hoping the whale could hear her. "Melae, welcome back!"

The boat docked, and Hallie followed the other passengers down the steps to the gangplank, so busy listening to the whale's whistling that she hardly noticed where her feet were taking her. Listening, she stepped onto the gangplank, but as she crossed it, the whistling stopped abruptly and was gone. All Hallie heard was the hollow echo of her own feet on the metal plank.

Hallie stopped short, and a man behind her carrying bags in both hands bumped into her. "Hey, watch out, little girl," he said in irritation.

Hallie stepped out of the way onto the pier, too astounded by the idea that had suddenly come to her to apologize. She had realized that every time she had heard the whale she had been on a boat or in the water—in the dinghy, in the ocean, on the ferry. And every time that abrupt silence had fallen, it had happened just as Hallie stepped back onto the land.

That's it! she said to herself. I'll bet that's it! I have to be on water to hear her. We can't talk when I'm on land! If she could run back onto the boat, she could test her theory. If she was right, she'd be able to hear Melae's whistling again as soon as she stepped back on the ferry.

But the crowds still streaming over the narrow gangplank were too thick. She wouldn't be able to squeeze past them onto the ferry, and anyway, the deckhands probably wouldn't let her.

"I'll just wait until everybody gets off," said Hallie out loud. "Then I'll run back onto the boat, just for a minute, and listen."

"Did you say something?" Her father was suddenly beside her, with both bags of groceries in his arms.

"Um, no, Dad," said Hallie, startled. "I was just talking to myself."

"Hmm." Her father peered at her quizzically over a bunch of celery. "I don't remember that you ever did that before. Well, come on, help me carry these up to the car. Let's get home."

"Just a minute, Dad, okay?" she asked. "There's something I have to do first."

"Hallie, I need help with these groceries," said her father, with some of his old firmness. "No matter what you may feel you have to do, I'm not about to carry them all up the hill to the Jeep by myself."

"Oh, Dad, can't it wait just a minute? This is important," begged Hallie.

"These bags are heavy," said her father. "What is it you have to do?"

"I can't explain." Hallie glanced back at the boat in agony. Only a few passengers still waited on the ferry to cross the bottlenecked gangplank. It wouldn't take long to unload them all. This boat was going down the bay to the other islands before it returned to the city, so nobody was waiting on the landing to climb aboard. That meant the ferry would pull away from the pier as soon as the last passenger disembarked. Hallie didn't have much time.

"Here, Dad, give me one of those," she said swiftly, and snatched a bag out of her father's arms. Clutching the heavy bag awkwardly, she ran across the pier and up the cobblestoned street. If she hurried, she might make it to the Jeep and back in time to test her theory.

It seemed to take forever to lug the heavy bag breathlessly up the steep bluff and find her way through the crowded parking lot, but at last she reached the Jeep. She yanked open the one door that worked and set the bag down on the seat so hurriedly that it tipped over, spilling oranges onto the floor. Hallie left it like that, turned and ran back down the hill, past her bewildered father trudging up with the other bag.

"Don't wait for me," she yelled back over her shoulder. "I'll walk home!"

The last passengers crossed the plank as she ran onto the landing, and the deckhands were already untying the ropes.

"Wait, wait," she shouted, running past the startled

deckhands, across the gangplank and back onto the boat.

She stopped short in the middle of the deck and listened, and there it was. That same glorious music filling her heart, that crazy, beautiful whistling, like a flute gone wild. She spread out her arms to the high, blue, September sky and laughed out loud.

"Hallie, what in the name of Pete has gotten into you, anyway?" It was Ira, standing in front of her, looking distinctly cross. "All day you've been acting weird. First you wouldn't get on the boat this morning, then you wouldn't get off. Now you did get off, and then you got back on. Have you gone nuts, or what?"

"No," said Hallie, with her widest, happiest smile. She just barely stopped herself from kissing Ira's confused brown face. "I'm fine, Ira. In fact, I've never been better. In fact, I'm great!"

"Well, anyway, get off the boat, would you?" said Ira, but he smiled back at her slowly, almost in spite of himself. "We have to get down the bay."

"Of course you do," said Hallie, still beaming. "Sorry. Bye!" Waving joyfully, she ran past Ira, who was shaking his head, and crossed the plank in one gleeful bound. The music in her head stopped as she landed on the dock, but she didn't care. She couldn't remember ever feeling happier in her life.

Hallie ran, singing, all the way home. She was pounding up the porch steps before it occurred to her that she could have gone straight to the beach, to see if she could hear Melae by wading in the ocean. She stopped with her hand on the doorknob, ready to run back down to the water. But before she could, her father's voice came through the screen door.

"Is that you, Hallie?"

Her father appeared in the shadows behind the screen.

"Why did you get back on the ferry?" he asked. "Did you forget something?"

"Um . . . yes. My backpack. I left my backpack on the boat and I had to go back for it." Maybe he just wouldn't remember that she'd had the pack on her back when she carried the grocery bag up to the Jeep.

"I thought it must be something like that," said her father vaguely. "Well, look, don't forget you've got to clean this kitchen floor. Those puddles made stains when they dried, and there's seaweed stuck to the floor. If your mother were here, she wouldn't like it very much."

Come on, Mom wouldn't care, Hallie thought rebelliously as she opened the screen door. Her mother, a pianist, had never paid as much attention to housekeeping as she did to her music.

But as she got out the mop, Hallie thought the kitchen did look as if it needed some kind of attention. Except for the stains on the floor, it was almost too neat. Without Josh's puzzle pieces scattered over the table, his blocks spilled on the floor, and his jelly smeared on the counter, the room looked bare. And it was too quiet. Hallie ran water hard into her bucket, trying to drown out the hollow sound of her own footsteps in the empty room.

It was hard to scrub off the grayish crust of dried salt left on the floor where her damp footprints had dried. Hallie shoved the mop over the floorboards, thinking about Melae again. The whistling music of the whale's song had been unlike anything she had ever heard, bigger than a bird's song, wild and free and wonderful. What did whales sing about? Was Melae sending some kind of message to the other whales when she sang like that? Or was she just making that wonderful noise for the joy of it, the way Hallie's mother played the piano in great crashing waterfalls of sound whenever she was happy?

As Hallie peeled a frond of seaweed off the floor and tossed it into the trash, she heard her father switch on the TV in the living room. "Hey, Dad," she called as she set the mop out on the porch to dry. "Do you know why whales sing?"

"Just a minute, Hallie, the news is on," her father

answered. "They're about to say something about the pilot whales, I think."

"They are?" Hallie let the screen door slam behind her and dashed into the living room.

On the television, an announcer gazed earnestly into the camera, with the harbor behind her. Her carefully curled hair didn't blow in the breeze that fluttered her skirt. "The Coast Guard spent the day trying to chase two pilot whales out of the harbor, but as evening fell, the Guard announced that it was giving up the effort. According to a spokesman, the Guard was able to drive the whales only a short distance away from the city before one of the whales, which seems to be injured, began to flounder and appeared to be unable to go any farther. The Guard reported that the other whale, which seems to be healthy, would not swim away from the injured one."

"Well, that's unfortunate," said Hallie's father, as she sat down next to him on the couch.

"The whales were first reported in the harbor early this morning by a city resident, who apparently thought they were submarines," the announcer went on. "Spectators crowded onto piers and into boats this morning to see the unusual visitors. Whale experts told Channel Nine that pilot whales sometimes beach themselves, a phenomenon known as stranding. The Coast Guard was attempting to prevent this behavior today by driving the whales into deeper water. But in spite of their efforts, this evening the whales were swimming back toward the city."

As she spoke, the announcer's face faded away,

replaced by a shot of choppy gray water. The camera moved in closer, and Hallie gasped as a gleaming bulge like a fat black melon burst suddenly through the sea. As a glossy fin rose dripping from the water behind the bulge, Hallie realized she was seeing the head and back of a whale. The camera pulled back to show two whales, side by side, crowded close together. One of the whales rested for a moment at the surface, its dorsal fin tilting listlessly to one side, but the other slipped below the sea in a gleaming black curve and came up again quickly on the other side of the resting whale, light shining on the black bulge of its head.

That must be Melae, thought Hallie in astonishment. From her big, musical voice, Hallie had imagined that Melae would be huge and graceful and lovely. But the whale on the TV screen was small and plump, and its bulging head had an almost clownish air. Still, as Hallie watched Melae's back lift once more into a lovely black arc before she vanished into the sea, she felt the corners of her mouth curving up in unreasonable delight.

"In other news, Governor Braxton announced new legislation today . . ." The picture shifted to a different announcer. Hallie's father clicked the remote control, silencing the television.

"Well, that's too bad," he said, sighing. "I hope the sick whale doesn't strand itself. If it does, the healthy one is likely to follow."

"Oh, she won't do that!" said Hallie quickly.

"I'm afraid they often do. And, anyway, how do you know the whale is female?" Her father blinked at her curiously.

"Oh . . . I don't, I guess," said Hallie uncertainly. She had assumed Melae was female, for some reason. But now that she stopped to think about it, she realized that she didn't know. "How can you tell with whales, Dad?"

"Well, it's just a guess, but by the shape of the dorsal fins, I'd say that you guessed right. The healthy one is female, and the sick one is probably a male. The males usually have a broader, larger fin."

"Why do they strand themselves, anyway?" Hallie asked. She couldn't imagine why a creature like Melae, who whistled so gladly and who spoke with so much joy and strength, would kill herself by swimming onto the shore. The scientists had to be wrong about it, somehow.

"Oh, there are a lot of theories. Sometimes it seems to be related to illness. But not all beached whales turn out to be sick. It might just be simple confusion. They're deepwater animals, and they don't seem to understand shallow water very well. Nobody really knows why it happens." Her father pushed his glasses up on top of his head. Exposed, his eyes were pale blue and exhausted.

"Why can't people just push the whales back in the water?" asked Hallie anxiously.

"Well, they do try," her father said. "There's a whole team of scientists and volunteers in New England who go to the scene when one of these strandings happens, to try to get the animals back into the water. But it doesn't always work. The whales weigh so much that their organs get damaged quickly on land, without the water to buoy them up. And even if people can get them back into the water, half the time they swim right back onto the beach."

"It doesn't make any sense," said Hallie.

"A lot of things in life don't make much sense, Hallie." Her father was staring across the room at the framed picture on her mother's piano of Josh and Hallie and their parents at the beach, taken on Josh's birthday earlier that summer. Josh sat on the sand, grinning widely, showing off the gap in his teeth where he had lost a front tooth that morning. He had been so thrilled to lose his first tooth on his birthday that he had almost cried.

Hallie looked away from the picture, away from her father's tired face, out the window overlooking the harbor. The sky was still full of light. She had time before sunset to take her father's binoculars down to the beach and see if she could catch a glimpse of the whales; time to wade into the water and listen for that wonderful whistling; time to try to speak to Melae again.

She got casually to her feet. "Dad, I'm going out for a walk," she said, in the most nonchalant voice she could manage. "I'll be back soon."

"Wait a minute, Hallie." Her father squinted at her with those naked-looking blue eyes. "We haven't had dinner yet."

Hallie wished her father would put his glasses back on. Without them, he looked too easy to hurt. "Can't we eat later?" she asked.

Her father put a hand on her shoulder. It shook slightly. Hallie tried to remember if his hands had always shaken like that. She didn't think they had.

"Look, why don't you just stay home tonight? I know

you're always eager to see Melissa, but I'd rather you stayed here," said her father.

"I'm not going to see Melissa," Hallie objected, but her father kept talking.

"Your mother's worried about you. She says you're worn out and upset, and I think she's right. You should get to bed early. You can see Melissa in the morning, can't you?"

"Oh, Dad, please . . ." Hallie took a breath to argue some more, but then she glanced up at her father and winced. The defenselessness of his eyes without his glasses and the way his hand quivered on her shoulder made her feel as if she ought to stay at home after all, as if she ought to take care of her father. It's not fair, she thought. Fathers are supposed to be strong. He ought to be taking care of me, not the other way around.

But she heard herself saying aloud, "Okay, okay. I'll stay in tonight." I'll just sneak out later, she promised herself. I'll wait until he goes to bed and then I'll climb out my window and slide down the shed roof and go down to the beach, the way I did this morning.

"Good." Her father patted her shoulder. "Now, what are we going to do about dinner?"

Hallie reluctantly followed him into the kitchen. Dinner would be easy, she thought. Just about everybody they knew on the island had brought casseroles after Josh got hurt. The refrigerator and freezer were stuffed full. Hallie and her father could probably eat for a month without cooking.

But when Hallie got into the kitchen, her father was

pulling a couple of orange cardboard cartons of frozen lasagna out of one of the still-unpacked grocery bags. They were shapeless and dripping, not frozen anymore after their long sojourn in the bag.

"Do you know what to do with these?" he asked helplessly. "Your mother bought them for us, but I'm not sure how to cook them."

"Oh, Dad, honestly, you just stick them in the microwave." Hallie took the boxes out of her father's hand. "Here, let me. Why don't you put the rest of that stuff away?"

No wonder her mother had so much trouble getting her father to share the cooking, she thought, if he couldn't even figure out the directions on a frozen dinner box. Hallie had overheard some noisy arguments between her parents about how anybody with advanced degrees in science could have difficulty boiling water.

Her father unloaded oranges into the refrigerator while Hallie put the trays of lasagna into the microwave and set the timer, neither of them talking. The whir of the oven filled the silent kitchen. It was too quiet, Hallie thought. Usually, classical music would be playing on the kitchen radio while her mother made busy, cheerful noises with the pots and pans and Hallie and her parents talked over their day. Josh would be jumping around, talking and singing and banging into things, and sooner or later her father would scold him for making too much noise. It was strange to want Josh's racket now, when Hallie had so often before wished her little brother would quiet down.

When the phone rang, jangling noisily in the quiet

room, they both jumped, like sleepers interrupted by an alarm clock. Hallie's father moved first to answer it.

"Hello? Oh, Helen, dear. How is Josh? . . . I see, good . . . and how are you, sweetheart?" It was amazing, Hallie thought. As soon as he heard her mother's voice, her father's voice had filled out, gotten back its old confident ring. Listening to her father now, Hallie couldn't remember why she had thought she needed to take care of him.

"Yes, Hallie's here," her father said into the phone. "We were just fixing dinner. She's fine. Just a bit tired, as you noticed. Don't worry about us, Helen, I'm taking care of things. . . . I know. We miss you both, too. I'll be there first thing in the morning. . . . Okay. I'll put her on." He took the phone away from his ear. "Hallie? Your mother wants to talk to you."

Hallie took the phone reluctantly out of her father's hand, which didn't seem to be shaking anymore.

"Hello?"

"Hello, darling. Feeling better now?" Her mother's voice seemed to fill the kitchen, as clear and strong as if she were standing beside Hallie.

"I'm fine, Mom. How's Josh?"

"He's doing okay, honey. He was so glad to see you this afternoon."

He hardly saw me at all, Hallie thought, but she said nothing. After a pause, her mother went on.

"Look, honey, tomorrow's Saturday, so you don't have school, and your dad's coming to the hospital in the morning. I don't want you to spend the day alone. Why don't I call Melissa's mother and ask her to expect you in the morning, after Dad goes up to town? You can spend the day with Melissa. Wouldn't that be nice?" Her mother's tone was coaxing, as if she were trying to cajole a very small child.

"I guess." Hallie heard the flatness in her own voice.

"You still sound so tired, darling, not like yourself at all," said her mother. "Please get to bed early, okay?"

Hallie interrupted. "Mom, why can't I come with Dad tomorrow? I still don't understand why I can't visit Josh."

Her mother's voice turned crisp. "Hallie, we've been through that already. There's nothing you can do for Josh right now."

"But, Mom . . ."

"No, Hallie, it's been decided, and that's enough. Now, Josh would like to speak to you. Shall I put him on?"

Hallie was so taken by surprise that for a moment she couldn't answer.

"Hallie?"

"Okay, Mom," she said then. "Yes, of course I want to talk to him."

"Let me just get the nurse to transfer the call to his room," said her mother.

She was calling 2from the nurses' station, so she could talk about Josh where he couldn't hear what she said, Hallie knew. Her mother had been doing that ever since Josh was admitted to the hospital.

There was a click in the line and then an empty sound. After all the energy in her mother's voice, the receiver sounded dead in Hallie's hands.

Then the line clicked again and Hallie thought she heard faint breathing.

"Josh?" she asked quickly.

After a pause, a small voice threaded through the line, so thin that Hallie hardly heard it. "Hi, Hallie."

Hallie frowned. This weak voice couldn't belong to Josh, her noisy little brother who shouted, slammed doors, never talked if he could yell, never walked if he could run. She pressed the receiver harder against her ear, as if to make him louder. "Joshie? Is that you?"

There was another pause. "It's me," said the voice uncertainly.

"How do you feel, Joshie?" asked Hallie.

"Okay." The small voice could have belonged to anybody, and it sounded so far away. Hallie thought suddenly of the telephone cable carrying her brother's voice under the harbor to the island, a skinny bundle of wires lying down there under tons of cold water and fish and seaweed. It seemed such a fragile connection. A stray anchor or a snag could snap the wires and cut him off from her, just like that. She blinked at an image that floated then, unbidden, into her mind—of the two whales, Melae and Globo, swimming through the water above the cable carrying her brother's voice.

"Josh, I have something to tell you," she said eagerly. "Something wonderful."

"What?" His voice sounded as young as a two-year-old's. And so tired, as if one or two words were all he could manage before he ran out of breath.

"I can't tell you now, Joshie. It's a secret. A surprise."

She waited for him to plead, to wheedle, to tease. Josh had always loved secrets. But the phone line buzzed with silence. Josh didn't speak.

"I'll tell you soon, okay?" said Hallie finally. "It's something really great."

"Okay, Hallie." Josh's small voice was dull. He didn't sound very interested. "Mom says to say bye now."

"Wait!" cried Hallie. "Josh . . . I miss you. I wish you were home. I hope you get better soon."

"Okay, Hallie. Bye." The threadlike voice was fading.

Hallie tried to say good-bye, but her voice wouldn't work. She hung on to the receiver, her eyes filling with hot tears. Talking to Josh hadn't felt like talking to Josh at all. It had been just like that afternoon in the parking lot, when all she could see was his dim hand and the distant white blur of a face that could have been anybody's behind the glass. She felt as if she hadn't been able to hear him over the phone, either, as if the glass were still between them.

Her mother's voice spoke through the phone in her ear. "Hallie? Are you there?"

Without answering, Hallie passed the phone back to her father and ducked out of the kitchen before he could see the tears spilling down her cheeks. One of Josh's red sneakers lay on the hall floor, and she snatched it up and hugged it as she ran up the stairs.

The sneaker was comforting, a small part of Josh. But Hallie wanted the whole person. She wanted her brother to tag along after her and tease her and annoy her, to make too much noise, to run up to her wearing his red sneakers, and she'd cross her eyes at him, the way she always did, and he'd stick out his tongue at her, the way he always did. Then he'd jump in her arms and knock her down so she could tickle him and make him giggle, until finally he kicked her in the shins and then she'd whack him with a sofa pillow and he'd pull her hair and they'd be fighting. That was what Hallie wanted, a good old-fashioned fight with her own tough, noisy, happy little brother. The boy on the phone hadn't sounded tough enough to fight with Hallie ever again.

She was halfway up the stairs when a thought stopped her so suddenly that her sobs dried up. Could Melae help Josh? Still clutching the sneaker, she stared into the darkness of the upstairs hall, frozen by the power of her own idea.

If Josh could hear Melae, if Melae could talk to him, wouldn't that help him get better? I bet it would, she thought in growing excitement. She's helping Globo, and he's sick or hurt or something. And she helped me when I fell in the water, so she can help people, too, not just whales. She could help Josh. She could lift him, or whatever it was she did for me when she saved me from drowning. Melae could make him happy again, Hallie thought with a sudden rush of hope. I know she could.

She turned around and ran back downstairs, where her father was just hanging up the phone.

"Dad, listen." She was so excited that her words tumbled over themselves. "Could Josh come out of the hospital for a little while tomorrow, for a boat ride?"

"A boat ride!" Hallie's father's eyebrows shot up behind his glasses. "Of course not."

"Just a short one?" begged Hallie.

"Hallie, no. What are you thinking of? You heard him on the phone just now. He's very weak, and he's in pain. He needs medication, and intravenous tubes, and he's very susceptible to infection. . . . No, honey, of course he can't go anywhere. He'll have to stay in the hospital for a while still."

"Oh." Hallie felt crushed with disappointment. She should have realized that Josh wouldn't be able to leave the hospital. But if she couldn't get him onto a boat, or into the ocean somehow, how could he speak with Melae?

The microwave timer buzzed. Her father opened the door and took out the two plastic pans of lasagna. "Time to eat."

Hallie put plates and silverware onto the table, thinking hard. If it would help Josh to speak with Melae, and she was sure it would, then she would just have to find some way for him to do it. There had to be a way. She would ask Melae about it that night, when she went down to the beach to talk to her after her father went to bed.

The lasagna was dried out and overcooked, because it had thawed and the time printed in the directions was for frozen lasagna. Hallie pushed it around the plate with her fork, but her father chewed on the tough pasta as if he didn't notice. He read the evening paper as they ate, holding it up like a wall between himself and Hallie. She was glad not to have to talk to him. She was too busy thinking, trying to figure out a way for Josh to speak with Melae.

She had sat there for quite a while before she realized she was looking at a headline on her father's newspaper that read, "Whales in the Harbor." Under it was a photograph. Hallie leaned across the table to get a better look. In the picture, a boat full of photographers was crowded close to two black shapes. The picture showed, more clearly than the television had, the rounded lines of the whales' backs, the soft curve of the dorsal fins, the glossy black surface of their skin. Their blowholes were like dimples in the center of their backs. They looked plump and soft and glossy, and the water flowed around them in soft curving rings.

"They're so beautiful," Hallie whispered to herself.

"Eh?" Her father put the paper down with a rattle. "Did you say something?"

"No, no," said Hallie, getting up. "Just talking to myself again. Look, Dad, you're right, I'm tired. I'm going upstairs to bed."

"Good idea." Her father smiled over the paper. "See you in the morning, dear. Sleep well."

"You, too," said Hallie. "Um, are you through with the front section?"

"Sure. Here, take it."

"Thanks. Good night, Dad." Hallie took the section with the photograph of the whales and escaped up the stairs. She wasn't really tired, she told herself. She just wanted to get off by herself, so that she could think in privacy. But she yawned as she hurried across the upstairs hall, past the closed door to Josh's room.

In the quiet darkness of her own room, the window framed the glittering lights of the city beyond the harbor. The dark water gave the city back its light in long, wavering, reflected stripes of white and red and gold. From here, the city looked enchanted, like a heap of jewels, as if nobody had ever been unhappy there.

The highest and brightest lights of all, on the very top

of the hill, were the lights of the hospital in a cold, white grid. Holding the newspaper with the photograph of the whales in her hand, Hallie stared out the window at the hospital.

"I'll do it somehow, Josh," she whispered. "I don't know how, yet, but I'm going to find a way for you to talk to Melae."

She set the newspaper down on her bedside table, folded so that the picture of the whales showed. Her bed looked soft and inviting. It seemed to be calling her. Hallie rubbed her eyes.

I'll just lie down for a little while, she thought. Just till I hear Dad go to bed. Then I'll get up, and go down to the harbor, and talk to Melae, and ask her about Josh. . . . Hallie interrupted her own thoughts with a yawn and lay down on her bed. The sleepiness that had overwhelmed her at the hospital suddenly engulfed her again. It had been such a long, long day.

Her pillow was soft, and it smelled like the lavender her mother kept in the linen closet. Lying there, Hallie tried to think about Josh and Melae. But all her thoughts seemed to run together into a blur. I'll just close my eyes for a second, she thought.

Hallie didn't even hear, some time later, her father's footsteps creaking up the stairs. She didn't move when her door swung gently open and light spilled across her face, or when her father carefully closed the door again and the dark returned. Beyond her window, the city lights winked out, one by one, and the whales swam through the dark water of the harbor while the stars swung silently across the huge, black, nighttime sky.

7

Something was buzzing in Hallie's ear. The buzzing droned into her dream, a wonderful dream that she was swimming with Melae in deep, clear water full of green light. She was underwater, but she could breathe easily, and swim as freely and joyfully as a gull flies. Side by side, she and Melae rose gladly through the crystalline green water. The whale was whistling, and her wild, exuberant piping filled Hallie's ears.

But the buzzing cut into her sleep, breaking up the music, destroying the dream. Whatever it was stopped buzzing and landed on her nose.

Half-awake, longing to swim back down into the sweet freedom of her dream, Hallie brushed the fly off her nose. It buzzed onto her chin. Crossly, she turned over, yanking her sheet over her head. But a memory was buzzing in her brain now, some vaguely remembered, painful thing, driving the wonderful dream farther into the shadows of sleep. It took Hallie a moment to remember what the bad thing was: Josh, of course, Josh not home, Josh hurt, Josh in the hospital.

The tight waistband of her jeans cut uncomfortably into her stomach, reminding her that she had never taken off her clothes the night before, that she had meant to get up and go out into the night. And then the memory of everything that had happened the day before flowed suddenly back. With a pulse of surprised delight that brought her fully awake, Hallie remembered Melae.

She threw back the sheet and sat up in bed. What time was it? Bright sunlight streamed in the window, falling in a golden pool on the rug. It was morning, Hallie realized, and fairly late morning at that, by the daffodil yellow of the light.

She squinted at her alarm clock. 8:30. It was late, all right, so late that her father must have left by now on the 8:15 ferry to go into town. Why hadn't he woken her up?

Hallie climbed out of bed and stretched, wincing at the soreness in her arms and back. Yesterday's struggle with the dinghy and the ocean had left her aching.

"Dad?" she called, but nobody answered. Frowning, she went out of her room and padded down the stairs.

The kitchen was quiet except for the dishwasher, humming efficiently through its cycle. A note in her father's spiky scrawl lay on the checked tablecloth. Hallie reached for a banana and peeled it absently as she read.

Hallie—I didn't want to wake you, since you were so tired last night. I called the Gianopouloses and told them you were sleeping late, so they won't expect you until lunchtime. I'll be in town all day. See you tonight. Love,

Dad

Hallie took a thoughtful bite of her banana. Nobody was home to ask awkward questions, and Melissa's family didn't expect her right away. She had fallen asleep before she could go down to the beach last night, but she had plenty of time to do it now. Briefly, she considered running back upstairs first to change out of her wrinkled, slept-in clothes. But then she caught a glimpse through the window of sunlight sparkling on the ocean, and decided not to bother. Popping the rest of the banana into her mouth whole, she ran across the kitchen and out into the morning.

Though the sun was bright, the air was cool, and the breeze carried a crisp scent of asters and bittersweet and autumn. Hallie ran across the yard to the path that led through a tangle of sumacs and wild roses to the steps at the top of the bluff. The last few pink roses bloomed bravely among the bright-red autumn rose hips.

The steps down to the beach were built of weathered gray wood, with a strip of black asphalt roofing tacked down the middle so that people with wet feet wouldn't slip. In summer, sometimes the roofing soaked up so much sun that it would burn bare feet, and people couldn't use the steps at all without shoes on. Today, even in the cool air of early fall, the asphalt was already warm under Hallie's bare soles.

She pounded down the steps, jumped off the flat rock at the bottom, and ran eagerly across the damp, cool sand to the waterline. Tangled heaps of seaweed, mussel shells, and plastic trash lay where the ocean had dumped them on the sand. A fisherman in high black waders stood in the water at the far end of the cove, and a white-haired woman in a sweat suit sat on a rock nearby, absorbed in a book. But it was early enough that the rest of the small beach was deserted. Mr. Gianopoulos's dinghy lay on the sand, drawn well up above the tide line and tied tightly with brand-new, sturdy, yellow rope. Hallie glanced at it guiltily and hurried past.

She looked eagerly out over the water, half expecting to find Melae there waiting for her. But except for a small flotilla of ducks bobbing near shore, the cove was empty. Sunlight glinted on the small waves of the cove, and at the end of the point, the surf crashed against Whaleback Rock. Across the channel, a lobster boat chugged along the rocky shore of Tourmaline Island, where old World War II fortifications, like squat, blocky castles, jutted up on the cliffs overlooking the ocean.

Hallie paused at the water's edge only long enough to roll up her jeans to her knees before she splashed eagerly in. But she stopped short when the chill knifed unexpectedly into her feet. Maine water never really got warm, and she was on the ocean side of the island, where the water was coldest of all.

She hesitated for a second, pulling one bare foot up out of the icy ripples. Maybe she ought to go over to Bayside Beach, on the city side of the island, where the harbor water lay warm and quiet under the sun like a giant bathtub. She'd actually be closer to the whales there, if they had gone back to the shipyard.

But that water would be greasy and polluted. Of course, it was all the same water, but somehow it seemed cleaner on the ocean side, where the view was of open sea and islands, not docks and city buildings and oil tankers, and where the tide rolled the green water into waves and splashed it onto the rocks in white cascades of salty foam.

And anyway, the cove was where Hallie had first spoken with Melae. She took a deep breath, steeled herself against the freezing ache spreading into the bones of her feet, and waded in deeper, until the icy water lapped against the rolled-up cuffs of her jeans.

"Melae?" She spoke softly, keeping her face turned away from the other people on the beach. "Melae? Can you hear me? Are you there?"

And as soon as she spoke, she felt the whale's presence rushing into her mind and body, as powerful as a wave, so warm and comforting and sure that the cold ebbed out of Hallie's feet.

SMALL ONE. The whale's voice echoed through Hallie's heart like some great, strange music. IT IS GOOD TO HEAR YOU AGAIN. WHERE HAVE YOU BEEN?

Hallie felt a smile spread across her face. Hugging herself to stop from jumping up and down and yelling with the sheer pleasure of hearing Melae's voice again, remembering to keep her voice down and her back turned to the other people on the beach, Hallie cried out softly, "I missed you, Melae! I've been right here, on the island. And at school, and at the hospital . . ."

She could tell that Melae didn't understand the words she was using; the whale's presence felt gently questioning, perplexed. After all, how would a whale know about schools or hospitals? Hallie struggled briefly to think of a way to explain them and realized she couldn't.

"I've been on land, Melae, that's why we couldn't speak to each other." Hallie's words fell over themselves in her eagerness to explain her discovery. She glanced over her shoulder at the other people on the beach, but they were paying no attention to her. "I figured it out. I can't speak to you—I can't hear you, either—when I'm on land. I have to be in the water, or in a boat . . . a shell, I mean . . . or we can't hear each other."

YES, said Melae. *IT IS ALWAYS SILENT, IN THE DRY PLACE.*

"The dry place? Is that what you call the land? It is dry, I guess. But it isn't really silent. It's kind of noisy, in fact." Hallie was babbling a little in her happiness. "But Melae, what about you? And Globo? Is he okay? My father said the Coast Guard . . . I mean, some people in shells . . . tried to chase you away."

The whale seemed to shudder. *SO MUCH NOISE,* she said. *IT HURT GLOBO. I COULD NOT HOLD HIM UP. I COULD NOT LISTEN TO KNOW WHERE TO GO.*

"Oh, Melae. It sounds awful."

WE TRIED TO SWIM AWAY, BUT THEY CHASED US. AND THEN GLOBO COULD NOT SWIM ANY-MORE.

"They were trying to help you, Melae," Hallie explained. "They didn't mean to scare you."

I TRIED TO TELL THEM THAT GLOBO NEED-ED REST. BUT THE LEGGED ONES NEVER LIS-TEN, EXCEPT FOR YOU.

"They can't hear you, Melae," said Hallie unhappily. "Most people can't hear whales. I never heard a whale talk before yesterday. I don't know why I can hear you now."

WELL, YOU ARE QUIET, FOR ONE THING, said Melae, in a distinctly grumpy tone. *THE OTHERS ARE SO NOISY. HOW CAN YOU LEGGED ONES LISTEN TO KNOW WHERE TO GO IN THOSE AWFUL SHELLS? WHY DON'T YOU GET LOST IN ALL THAT NOISE?*

"People don't get lost in noise. At least, I don't think we do." Hallie frowned uncertainly, thinking of the school hallways between classes, bewildering in their racket of laughter, yelling voices, the thumping of hundreds of feet, slamming locker doors, buzzing classroom bells. Lost was exactly how she felt in all that noise. "Well, anyway, people don't listen to go places. We use our eyes to see where to go. Don't you?"

EYES! The feel of the whale rippled, as though she were laughing. *EYES ARE NOT FOR GOING. WE SWIMMERS GO BY LISTENING.*

"But how do you do that?" Hallie asked. "What do you listen to?"

WE SING, explained the whale. *THE ECHOES OF OUR SONGS COME BACK TO US, AND TELL US WHERE TO GO. AND WE LISTEN TO THE OTHER SONGS.*

"What other songs?"

EVERYTHING UNDER THE SEA IS SINGING.

Hallie smiled. "I heard you singing yesterday. It was beautiful. You sounded so happy, Melae."

IT WAS ONE OF THE GLAD SONGS, FOR GLOBO. BECAUSE HE WAS TIRED, said Melae.

"Globo!" said Hallie guiltily. In the pleasure of speaking with Melae, she had forgotten about the sick whale for a few minutes. Remembering was like a shadow over the sun, like remembering Josh that morning after the blissful happiness of her dream. "Did your singing help, Melae? Is Globo getting better?"

HE IS VERY TIRED. Melae's big voice was sad.

"Melae, why can't I talk to Globo? Why can't I hear him, the way I hear you?" asked Hallie.

I DO NOT KNOW, admitted the whale. *HE SAYS HE DOES NOT HEAR YOU, EITHER.*

Hallie remembered the way the smaller whale had lolled at the surface when she had seen them on television, his dorsal fin tipped sadly to one side. "What's wrong with him, Melae?"

There was a pause, as if the whale were deciding how to explain. *HE CANNOT SING THE SONGS,* Melae said finally. *HE WAS HIT BY A SHELL, AND NOW HE SINGS ONLY THE FEAR SONG.*

"Is he going to get better?" Hallie asked.

I THINK SO, IN TIME. UNTIL THEN, I WILL LIFT HIM.

"How do you do that, anyway?" Hallie asked. "When you spoke to me yesterday, you made me stronger somehow. But you weren't touching me. You weren't anywhere near me. What did you do?"

I LIFTED YOU, said the whale simply.

"But what *is* that?"

There was a silence. *IT DOES NOT GO INTO SPEAKING,* said the whale finally.

Hallie thought for a moment before she spoke again.

"What would happen to Globo if you didn't keep lifting him, Melae?" But she had already guessed the answer.

HE MIGHT DROWN. OR HE MIGHT SWIM UP INTO THE DRY PLACE, AND NOT COME BACK, said Melae.

Melae and Hallie were quiet for a moment. Hallie could feel the whale's presence, even when she didn't speak. The silence between them seemed to rush with sound, like the whispering of a seashell held to her ear, or the rush of a wave toward the shore before it breaks on the rocks. Hallie wished she could see the whale, but from where she stood, the island blocked her view of the harbor. Only a few tall city buildings beyond the harbor jutted above the rooftops and the oak trees. Tallest of all was the glass and steel block of the hospital, dominating the skyline.

"Melae . . ." began Hallie hesitantly. "I know somebody who's hurt, like Globo. I wanted to ask if you would try to help him."

There was a pause. HOW COULD I HELP?

"I thought maybe you could speak to him," said Hallie. "And lift him, maybe, the way you lifted me."

The rushing of silence grew uncertain. I HAVE NEVER SPOKEN WITH A LEGGED ONE, BEFORE YOU, the whale said. I DO NOT KNOW IF HE WILL HEAR ME.

"Oh, he'll hear you," promised Hallie. "If I can hear you, he can, too. I'm sure of it. The problem is, I don't know yet how to get him down to the water. But if I can think of a way, will you try to speak with him?"

I WILL TRY, said the whale doubtfully. BUT WHAT

*IS WRONG WITH THIS LEGGED ONE? IS HE
SINGING THE FEAR SONG?*

"No," said Hallie. "Well, maybe something like that.
He's hurt, Melae, and I want to help him, but I can't.
He's my brother."

BROTHER? asked the whale. *WHAT IS THAT?*

"He's in my family," Hallie tried to explain. "Don't
you have families? He lives with me . . . he swims with
me, I guess you might say. He's little, Melae."

AH, A SMALL ONE, LIKE YOU.

"Smaller than me. His name is Josh." Hallie glanced
anxiously across the beach at the fisherman and the
woman with her book. They were still paying no attention. As she watched, the woman turned a page.

AND HOW IS YOUR JOSH HURT?

Hallie swallowed before she said, uncomfortably, "He
got burned."

I DO NOT KNOW THIS BURNED. The whale's
voice was puzzled.

"You know, burned. Hurt by a fire," said Hallie, a little
impatiently.

BUT WHAT IS FIRE? Now the whale sounded curious, like a child who has run across a new word in a
book.

"Oh." Hallie paused. Of course Melae didn't know
about fire. There was no fire underwater. A whale would
never get burned. How could Hallie explain it? She took
a deep breath.

"Fire is very hot, Melae. It burns. Like . . . maybe like
a huge jellyfish sting, or something. It destroys things. It

can do good things, too, like keeping people warm, or cooking food, but if it touches you, it hurts your skin."

I DO NOT UNDERSTAND, said Melae regretfully.

"I guess I'm not explaining it very well. But, anyway, Melae, will you help him?"

I WILL TRY, SMALL ONE. BUT I AM AFRAID THAT I MAY NOT BE ABLE TO HELP THIS . . . WHAT DID YOU CALL HIM? THIS JOSH.

"But, Melae, why not?" Hallie's startled voice rose louder than she meant it to, and across the beach, the white-haired woman glanced up briefly from her book.

THIS BURNING IS A THING OF THE DRY PLACE, NOT OF THE SEA, SMALL ONE. MAYBE I CANNOT HELP.

"But you can, I know you can! Melae, you have to!" Hallie's voice echoed across the cove. The reading woman glanced up again, and the fisherman stared curiously across the water at Hallie. Impatiently, Hallie turned away and lowered her voice. "You helped me, Melae!"

BUT YOU WERE IN THE SEA, SMALL ONE. I KNOW THE SEA. THIS BURNING . . . I DO NOT KNOW ABOUT THIS.

"But, Melae . . ." pleaded Hallie. "He needs help so badly. If you don't help him, who will?"

The whale did not answer, and the whispering seashell silence fell again.

"Melae!" shouted Hallie. "Aren't you listening to me?"

The white-haired woman put a finger in her book to mark her place. "Little girl, are you all right?" she called. "Who are you shouting at?"

Hallie paid no attention. "Melae, are you still there?"

But the quality of the whale's presence was changing. When she spoke again, she sounded anxious and distracted. *THOSE SHELLS AGAIN,* she said. *TOO CLOSE . . . TOO LOUD . . .*

"Melae?" asked Hallie, alarmed. "What's going on?"

I CANNOT HEAR YOU, SMALL ONE, said the whale. *TOO MUCH NOISE . . .* Her voice was fading, and with it, the comforting sense of her presence ebbed away from Hallie like the tide washing away from the shoreline.

"Melae? Come back!" called Hallie anxiously. But the whale's presence had vanished as completely as it had when Hallie stepped off the ferry. She stamped a cold foot in frustration and almost fell, as pain shot through it like hundreds of icy needles.

"Melae!" Hallie called again, but nobody answered.

Hugging her elbows close to her, half crying with frustration, Hallie turned back toward the shore. And there at the waterline, long hair blowing in the wind, stood Melissa, her head cocked sideways as she stared curiously at Hallie.

"Hallie, what are you doing in that cold water?" she asked, with her crinkle-nosed, friendly grin. "And who in the world were you talking to just now?"

Speechless, Hallie stared at Melissa. Then she glanced up at the trees blocking her view of the harbor. If only she could see what was happening to the whales!

"Hallie?" asked Melissa nervously.

Hallie realized that she was scowling. She blinked, smoothed out her face, and tried to smile at Melissa. "Hi," she finally managed to get out.

"Hi." Melissa smiled back, a bit uncertainly. "What are you doing in the water? Aren't you freezing?"

"Oh, no." Hallie tried to sound nonchalant, although in fact the icy cold was seeping up her legs, and her frozen feet were sending her urgent messages to get them back onto dry, warm land. "The water's not very cold. I was just . . . um . . . wading a little. Trying to cool off."

Melissa frowned. "It isn't hot out."

Hallie splashed out of the icy water onto the beach, trying not to look as if she was hurrying. The sand was blessedly warm under her shriveled toes, but the breeze was cold on her wet legs. She couldn't keep herself from shivering.

"You're freezing, you idiot. Here, take my sweater."

Melissa pulled off her cardigan and handed it to Hallie, who gratefully tugged it on.

"Who were you talking to?" Melissa asked again.

Hallie pulled the sweater close and forced a laugh, rubbing one foot against the other calf to try to warm it. "I guess I must have been talking to myself."

Melissa squinted at Hallie. "Are you sure you're feeling all right, Hallie? I mean, sometimes crazy people talk to themselves."

"I am not crazy, Melissa!" Hallie snapped. But privately, she wondered. Maybe the whale wasn't really talking to her. Maybe she was losing her mind, and she just didn't know it yet.

"Well, I just wondered," Melissa said. "You've been acting awfully strange lately. Anyway, I thought you were going to come over to my house when you got up. What are you doing down here?"

Hallie scowled down at her white, wrinkled feet. She didn't want to go to Melissa's. She wanted to find out what was happening to the whales. Melae had sounded so frightened, all of a sudden. What could have happened?

"Hallie? Is something wrong?" asked Melissa. "You look so worried."

Melissa's friendly voice was so familiar and comforting that, for a moment, Hallie was tempted to tell her everything. Melissa was her oldest friend, after all. Maybe she would understand.

But as Hallie hesitated, the distant blare of the ferry horn floated across the harbor. Suddenly, Hallie realized that from the ferry, she would be able to see what was happening to Melae and Globo. If she left now and ran all the way to the landing, she just might get there in time to catch the boat.

"Melissa, listen," she said quickly. "I can't come over to your house yet. There's something important I have to do first."

"What is it?" asked Melissa.

"I can't explain right now," said Hallie. "Look, don't tell your mother you saw me, so she'll think I'm still sleeping. I'll get to your house pretty soon. Please?"

Melissa's face was creased with confusion. "Well, okay, I guess. But, Hallie, what's going on?"

Hallie wished she could see how far away the ferry was. Did she still have time to catch it? She began to trot toward the steps, calling back over her shoulder, "Melissa, I've got to go now, okay?"

"Wait, I'll come with you!" Melissa shouted after her.

"No, no, let me go alone. I'll explain later, I promise." Hallie ran across the beach and up the steps, her bare feet echoing on the wooden treads.

At the top, she glanced back down. Melissa stood on the beach where Hallie had left her, a small figure against the wide backdrop of cove and islands and ocean. Hallie waved, but Melissa stood with her hands at her sides, staring up at Hallie. After a minute, Hallie turned away from her and ran down the path.

She pounded past her house, wishing she could stop to grab her shoes. But if she did that, she might miss the ferry. She kept running.

The one-minute warning had not yet sounded as Hallie ran breathlessly down the hill to the ferry landing, bruising her bare feet on the cobblestones. She had made it with time to spare. The passengers were still waiting on the dock, while the deckhands painstakingly directed a line of waiting cars into place on the open deck of the car ferry, a flat boat like a floating parking lot which carried vehicles between the islands and the city.

Waiting with the others, still out of breath, Hallie shifted her weight impatiently from one stinging bare foot to another. She would have had time to stop at home for her shoes after all. She wished she had.

Waiting, she craned her neck to stare across the harbor. In the distance, she could make out a commotion of boats crowded together near the shipyard, but they were too far off for her to see clearly. Once she was on the ferry she could try again to speak to Melae. Maybe by now the whale would be able to hear her again.

When the last car was parked and the deckhands beckoned to the waiting passengers, Hallie ran aboard, staying well away from the deckhands. Bare feet weren't allowed on the ferry. If the deckhands saw that she didn't have her shoes, they wouldn't let her on the boat.

Most of the other passengers mounted the narrow stairs to the passenger cabin in the wheelhouse, perched like a tree house above the open deck where the cars were parked. But Hallie stayed downstairs on the deck, standing between a parked station wagon and a van, listening for the voice of the whale.

"Melae?" she whispered. "Can you hear me now?"

As the horn sounded and the ferry plowed away from the dock, Hallie stood still, listening. But all she heard was the churning engine and the high, shrill cries of the gulls overhead. She could feel no hint of the presence of the whale. Whatever was going on across the bay, Melae still could not hear her, or at least could not answer.

Anxiously, Hallie made her way between the parked cars to the bow. Though the ferry had chest-high metal sides, it was open across the bow and the stern so that cars could drive on and off. The deck where Hallie stood rode only a few feet above the harbor, and nothing separated her from the water but a strip of nylon rope netting lashed across the opening.

As the ferry picked up speed, the green water churned, splashing back over Hallie in a cold salt spray. She buttoned Melissa's sweater, leaned against the warm hood of a parked car, and let the spray blow in her face while she gazed across the harbor, trying to see what was happening to the whales.

But the car ferry had chugged its slow, laborious way almost all the way to the city before it got close enough to the cluster of boats by the shipyard for Hallie to see them clearly. They were so crowded together that they made her think of pictures she'd seen in her history books of covered wagons circling together on the prairies. Sailboats, motorboats, yachts, and even a few lobster boats were jostling with one another, all trying to get close to something Hallie couldn't see in the water. The boats tipped toward the inside of the circle as the people in them crowded along the sides, staring, pointing cameras, waving, shouting.

In the center of the circle must be Melae and Globo,

of course, but Hallie couldn't see them. Were they okay? Hallie closed her eyes and whispered again. "Melae? Melae! What's going on?" But no answer came.

Hallie stared at the jumble of boats till her eyes hurt, struggling for a glimpse of Melae and Globo. But there were too many boats too close together, and the captain was keeping the car ferry well away from the confusion. Mack wouldn't take the ferry over to give the passengers a look at the whales on this trip. The clumsy car ferry would be too hard to maneuver through a crowd of boats like that. And from this distance, try as she might, Hallie couldn't see anything but boats.

But the noise! After what Melae had said about noisy motors, Hallie heard the whining roar of all those boat engines in a way she never had before. They throbbed like angry bees. It must be even worse, carried through the water to the sensitive whales, thought Hallie. It must be driving them crazy. What was happening to them? How could Melae keep on lifting Globo in all this racket?

As the car ferry steamed steadily along, a teenager perched in the bow of an overloaded motorboat shouted, "The whales are over this way, Dad! I can see them!" The boat veered and cut deftly into the crowd. Another, larger boat buzzed past the ferry, emblazoned CHAN-NEL NINE. From its bow, a woman with a video camera was filming the commotion. Hallie stood on tiptoe and craned her neck desperately, but she was too far away. She could not see the whales.

Half crying with frustration, Hallie whispered,

"Melae! What's going on? Are you all right?" And unexpectedly, a brief, uncertain response crackled through her mind, like a radio station half-choked with static.

TOO NOISY. TOO CLOSE. . . . An onrush of panic drenched Hallie like a cold wave as the whale spoke raggedly in her mind. And then, as quickly as it had come, the whale's presence vanished.

"Melae! Talk to me! Come back!" cried Hallie, but the whale did not answer.

Before she knew she was going to say anything, Hallie found herself screaming across the water at the circus of boats. "Go away! You're scaring the whales! Go away and leave them alone!"

But the droning of engines drowned her out. Her heart still pounding from the panic and confusion she had sensed in the whale, Hallie banged a frustrated hand on the hood of the car she had been leaning on, earning a glare from its driver riding inside.

A siren wailed across the water, and the black-and-white harbor police launch zipped past the ferry. Among the people crowded on its rear deck, Hallie thought she saw her father's tall, hunched shape. She put a hand over her eyes to block the glare of the sun and squinted. Sure enough, there was her father, pointing to where the whales must be, talking to someone at his side. What was he doing out with the harbor police? He was supposed to be visiting Josh.

"Dad!" shouted Hallie. She cupped her hands around her mouth and screamed. *"Dad!"*

Her father didn't turn. Hallie leaned over the nylon

netting, ignoring the cold spray splashing into her face, yelling for all she was worth. "Dad! Get the boats away! They're hurting the whales! Make them go away!"

But the wind grabbed her voice away, and the car ferry chugged steadily toward the city, widening the distance between Hallie and her father. "Dad!" Hallie shrieked in frustration. "You've got to listen!" But her father's back stayed turned. As Hallie watched, the police boat's siren whooped again, and it cut past the lobster boat into the middle of the knot of boats, where Hallie could no longer see it.

Hallie chewed on a finger in exasperation. If only she had a radio, so she could talk to her father and explain. A radio! The ferry had one, upstairs in the wheelhouse. Maybe she could talk the captain into letting her use it.

Quickly, Hallie threaded her way back through the parked cars toward the stern. She ran up the narrow steel stairs, clutching the handrail for balance as the ferry rocked over a motorboat wake. At the top, she ran across the open landing and burst into the wheelhouse, banging its steel door against the wall.

"Mack!" she shouted at the captain, who stood at the wheel, silhouetted against the windshield, his back turned to Hallie. "Can I use your radio?"

The captain jumped and turned around. "Hallie Rainsford! What in blazes are you banging my door for? Scared me out of a year's growth."

"Oh . . . sorry," said Hallie distractedly. "I didn't mean to bang it. But I need to use your radio, Mack. It's an emergency."

"An emergency! On my ferry?" Mack frowned. "What's going on?"

"It isn't on the ferry," Hallie tried to explain. "It's about those whales. I . . . I can't really explain how I know this, Mack, but all those boats are so close, they're scaring the whales. My dad's on the police boat, and I need to tell him that Globo's sick, and if Melae can't lift him, he might drown. . . ."

"Hold it, hold it." Mack lifted a hand to cut off the stream of Hallie's frightened words. "I don't know who Globo is, or what this is all about. But my radio's not for passenger use, Hallie."

"But this is important!"

Mack shook his head with decision. "Nope. Sorry."

"But, Mack . . ." wailed Hallie.

The captain interrupted, frowning down at Hallie's dirty bare feet. "Hey, where are your shoes? No bare feet allowed on this ferry, young lady."

Hallie had forgotten about her bare feet. She backed away a step. "Um, I left my shoes downstairs."

Mack sighed. "Well, go put 'em on, and leave 'em on, and stay out of here for the rest of the trip, will you? I've got a ferry to run, and I can't do it with you bugging me."

"But, Mack . . ." Hallie tried once more, but the captain's scowl turned fierce.

"Scoot!" he said. Hallie backed out of the wheelhouse as the captain closed the door with a firm click.

Tears stung Hallie's eyes as she stood on the landing. Why wouldn't Mack listen? What was she going to do?

Then she realized that from up here at the top of the

stairs, she could see over the jostling yachts and speed-boats into the center of the circle. There, plunging up and down in the foamy water, were two gleaming black forms. Hallie grabbed the railing and stared.

The whales were milling around in a small circle, coming up to breathe and then diving again, jostling each other in the small stretch of open water. Small clouds of steam puffed out of their blowholes each time they emerged.

Even from so far away, Hallie could see that the surface of the smaller whale's skin was grayish and pocked with scars, and he hesitated at the surface before diving listlessly again. Even to Hallie's inexperienced eyes, he looked sick. But the larger whale gleamed glossy black. As Hallie watched, Melae flicked her tail, sending a contemptuous shower of water flying at a boat that had cut so close it nearly ran over Globo. There was a lilt in the curve of her back that looked to Hallie just the way Melae sounded, almost as if she were laughing as she swam.

"Melae!" shouted Hallie. "Melae, I see you! Melae, hello!" But no answering voice spoke in her mind. She squinted as Melae's bulging black head burst through the surface again, trying to see the whale's face. But from above, Hallie could see only the glossy oval of her back and fin against the rough gray water.

A thin siren rose from the cluster of boats. It came from the harbor police launch, working its way along the inner rim of the circle. Slowly, Hallie realized that it was forcing the boats back, driving them away from the whales. She could see her father holding up a megaphone; she could hear its tinny squawking above the drone of the engines, but she was too far away to understand what he was saying. Reluctantly, the circle of boats was falling away, opening a stretch of silver sea around the whales.

Her father *was* trying to help the whales, she realized. That's why the harbor police were out there. The open water around the whales was growing steadily wider as the boats dropped reluctantly away. Hallie's knees went suddenly weak with relief, and she clutched the railing for balance.

"Oh, thank you, Dad," she whispered, staring down at the larger whale, whose movements seemed a little calmer already. Surely the whale would be able to talk to her now. "Melae? Can you hear me now? Are you okay?"

But the two whales continued to jostle anxiously against each other. No answer came. As Hallie stared helplessly, the ferry swung into its last turn around the shipyard pier. The warehouse on the pier slipped between Hallie and the harbor, blocking her view of the whales.

"Melae? What's happening? Are you okay?" she whispered once more.

There was still no answer. A thump shook the deck under Hallie's feet as the ferry bumped against the dock. As the deckhands tied it into place and lowered the ramp, the passengers crowded out of the cabin behind Hallie. To get out of their way, she had to climb down the stairs to the lower deck, where the deckhands shooed her off the ferry along with the rest of the passengers.

Hallie winced as she walked off the ramp onto the graveled surface of the pier. She stepped carefully over sharp stones and shards of glass as the other passengers hurried up the pier toward the city.

I'll get right back on this boat and take it back to the island, Hallie thought as the first car rolled past her off the ferry, its wheels crunching on the gravel. I'll ride back across the harbor, and stay up on the landing this time so I can see. Even if I can't do anything to help the whales, at least I can keep an eye on them, and I'll be back on Garnet before Melissa's mother starts to wonder where I am.

That was when Hallie remembered that she didn't have a ferry ticket. She hadn't needed one to come over, because tickets weren't collected on the island. But nobody could get on the ferry in the city without a round-trip ticket. Hallie searched the pockets of her jeans, but they were empty. Her wallet, with her student commuter tickets and her money tucked inside, was in her school backpack, forgotten at home in a corner of the kitchen.

Maybe Melissa had a ticket or some money in her sweater. Hallie searched feverishly through its pockets, but turned up only a barrette, a crumpled tissue, and a penny.

"What do I do now?" asked Hallie out loud, but her only answer was the raucous screech of a gull overhead, like mocking laughter. All by herself in the city with no tickets, no money, and no shoes, Hallie stood, bewildered, on the pier. On top of everything else, she was getting hungry. What was she going to do?

The last car had driven off the ferry before Hallie remembered the spare boat tickets her mother kept in the glove compartment of the mainland car for emergencies just like this. If she could find the car, and if it wasn't locked, she could use one of the spare tickets to get home. Her father must have parked it somewhere near the waterfront before he went out on the police boat.

She'd have to hurry, though, if she wanted to find the car in time for the return trip back to Garnet. The ferry was scheduled to leave in fifteen minutes, and the next one didn't leave until noon. If she had to wait for that one, she'd be very late getting to Melissa's.

The first place to check was her family's space in the parking garage. Watching for broken glass and gull droppings, Hallie picked her way across the pier into the garage and ran up the cool, oil-stained concrete ramp to the second floor. But her family's parking space was empty.

"Drat. Where is it?" Hallie's voice echoed in the dim depths of the garage. I really am starting to talk to myself a lot, she thought uneasily, as she ran back down the ramp and out into the harsh sunlight of the pier.

An old, black pickup truck loaded with lumber rolled past Hallie toward the ferry as she trotted around the corner onto Waterfront Street. The brick sidewalk was warm and almost soft under her bare feet. She ran along the street, searching among the parked cars for her family's red station wagon.

Waterfront Street had once been the heart of the city's fishing district. Now Hallie dodged through crowds of tourists wandering among the craft shops, gourmet delicatessens, and expensive boutiques that filled the old brick buildings where fish markets used to be. Her family's familiar station wagon was nowhere to be seen among the sleek cars with out-of-state license plates that lined the cobblestoned street. Horns honked impatiently as Hallie ran across the street through the snarled traffic, stubbing her big toe sharply on a cobblestone.

"Ouch!" she yelped, hopping on the good foot. A woman beside her, loaded down with shopping bags, glanced at Hallie's dirty bare feet in startled disapproval.

But just then, Hallie spotted the car, parked half a block away on the waterfront side of the street, by the flight of steps that led down to the police boat landing. She dodged around the woman with her bags and back across the street. Now, if her father had just forgotten to lock the car, the way he often did, everything would be fine.

She had made it to the car and was standing in the street, her hand on the driver's door, when she heard her father's voice.

"Maybe those whales ought to be separated."

Hallie ducked down beside the car. Through its tinted windows she could see her father coming up the steps from the police boat landing, his hair standing on end from the wind, talking to a young man whom Hallie vaguely recognized as one of his lab assistants from the university.

"Oh, great," muttered Hallie in frustration. The police boat must have just docked. What awful timing! She couldn't let her father see her. She was supposed to be home on Garnet, sleeping late. She could think of no way to explain what she was doing in the city, in her bare feet, without even a ticket home. Staying crouched to keep the car between herself and her father, Hallie half crawled toward the back of the car, looking for a place to hide.

As he climbed the stairs, her father was still talking. "The harbor police can keep all those boats at a safe distance from the whales now. But as long as they're together, both those animals are still at risk."

The lab assistant spoke. "I don't know. Looks to me as if that smaller whale's a little stronger today than he was yesterday. Maybe he's recovering. Maybe if we just leave them alone, they'll go back out to sea on their own."

"Well, the team from the aquarium will have to decide that when they get here." Her father's voice was its old, loud, confident self. "But the sick one probably won't get better. They hardly ever do. And if it does beach, you know the healthy one will go with it. I think the only way to protect the healthy one is to split them up."

Hallie froze, crouched by the rear fender. Her father

was talking about separating Melae and Globo. But didn't he realize that without Melae, Globo might die?

Her father was on the sidewalk now, standing by the car on the passenger side. His car keys jingled as he pulled them out of his pocket. Any second now, he would come around to Hallie's side of the car to get in.

She looked around desperately. Where could she hide? The street was clogged with cars, whose drivers glanced at her curiously as they passed. If she stood up to try to cross, her father would see her. But he was on the sidewalk, only six feet away. She couldn't go that way, either.

There was only one thing to do. Still crouching, Hallie darted across the space between her father's car and the blue sedan parked behind it, suppressing a cry of pain as she stepped on something sharp. Then, trying not to imagine what the drivers who saw her were thinking, she waddled along between the street and the blue sedan and ducked behind it, just in time, as her father walked around the front of their car.

Safely out of her father's sight, Hallie squatted in the grit and trash littering the street, staring at speckles of rust and a sticker boasting THIS CAR CLIMBED MOUNT WASHINGTON on the car's bumper.

Her father's voice carried over the traffic. "Driving the healthy whale away from the sick one might at least save her," he was saying.

"Hey, Hallie, what are you doing down there? Did you lose a contact lens or something?" This voice didn't belong to Hallie's father. It came from right beside her.

Dismayed, she looked up. Ira stood on the sidewalk, grinning down at Hallie in friendly inquiry.

"Shhhh!" she pleaded in a frantic whisper. "Don't let my dad know I'm here!"

Ira's face was puzzled, but as Hallie put a finger over her lips imploringly, he rolled his eyes and shrugged in bemused agreement. Hallie's father was saying to the graduate student, "I'm on my way up to the hospital now to visit my son. Climb in, and I'll drop you off at the lab on my way."

"How is your son, anyway?" asked the assistant, but the car doors slammed shut before Hallie heard her father's reply. She sagged against the blue car's bumper in relief as the station wagon's engine roared to life and her father drove away.

Ira's arms were folded as he gazed down at Hallie. "All right, he's gone, so come clean. What the heck are you doing? And where are your shoes?"

Hallie stood up slowly, her mind racing. "I . . . um . . . I lost my shoes. I was hiding from my father because . . . um . . . because he'll be mad if he finds out I lost them. They were a brand new pair." She glanced hopefully at Ira. Had he believed her?

Ira's eyebrows were raised so high that they had disappeared under his curly hair. "You lost your shoes? How'd you do that?"

Hallie stared at him blankly for a moment. "Um . . . well . . . I got them wet in a puddle," she improvised. "So I had to take them off. And then I put them down someplace, only I don't remember where. So now, I have to catch this boat home to get another pair before my Dad finds out." Hallie felt startled and somewhat pleased by her own powers of invention.

"Where did you find a puddle?" Ira asked with interest. "It hasn't rained in days."

"I . . . I don't remember," said Hallie lamely.

Ira stared at her for a minute. Then he threw back his head and let out a shout of laughter. "Boy, you are some weird kid," he said. "Look, I don't know what you did with your shoes, or why you were hiding from your dad, and I don't care. But you better have something on your feet. I've got a pair of flip-flops in my locker, down at the ferry office. Want to borrow 'em?"

"Okay," said Hallie in a small voice.

"Come on, then," said Ira, and Hallie followed him meekly, limping a little, down the pier to the ferry landing and into the small, dark office behind the ticket window. She saw with relief that the car ferry was still tied up at the dock. A truck loaded with propane gas tanks was rolling carefully into place on the deck.

Ira swung open his locker door and produced a very large, well-worn pair of blue rubber flip-flops. "They might be a bit big," he said, handing them to her. "But they're better than nothing."

Hallie stepped into them. The soft rubber felt wonderful under her bruised, tired feet, even if the soles did extend several inches past the ends of her heels.

"These are great. Thanks a lot, Ira," she said.

"Think nothing of it, ma'am." Ira swept her a mock bow. "Now, do you need anything else?"

"Um . . . well . . . could I maybe borrow a boat ticket?" asked Hallie, abashed.

Ira's eyebrows disappeared again. "You lost your tickets, too? Don't tell me, you dropped 'em in the puddle with your shoes, right?"

Hallie stared dumbly at Ira, unable to think of anymore excuses. But he was grinning at her, his white teeth brilliant against his tanned skin. "Look, don't worry about it. I'm working this boat. I'll let you on, and you can give me an extra ticket next time you come across."

"Thanks," mumbled Hallie.

"Think nothing of it, like I said. Hey, I like weird people. You keep life interesting. But now, if I don't run, I'm going to be late to work."

With that, Ira slammed shut his locker and sprinted off toward the ferry. Hallie shuffled after him as fast as she could. The flip-flops were so large that she had to squeeze her toes around the thongs to keep them from falling off. By the time she got to the boat, the cars had finished loading and the passengers were getting on. Ira stood by the ramp taking tickets. He winked as Hallie flapped past him onto the ferry.

As the boat steamed slowly along the pier toward the open water of the harbor, Hallie tried to climb the steel stairs to the landing. But the flip-flops caught on the steps, making her stumble. She pulled them off, climbing the steps in bare feet, and bent quickly to thrust the flip-flops back on as soon as she reached the top, glancing guiltily at the wheelhouse. Through the window in the door, she could see Mack, his back turned as he concentrated on piloting the ferry.

"Melae?" whispered Hallie into the breeze, staring past the end of the pier, wishing the boat would move faster out into the open water of the harbor so she could see the whales. "Melae? Are you okay now? Can you hear me?"

But before she could listen for an answer, a human voice spoke from the open door of the passenger cabin behind her. "Hallie Rainsford, I'm so glad to see you. Come in here and sit by me," someone called. "Tell me how your brother is doing. Come sit down, dear."

Hallie turned reluctantly. Mrs. Gladding, the minister's wife, was smiling and firmly patting a space on the bench beside her. There was no way to avoid going to sit with her, no way to escape her friendly, concerned questions about Josh and Hallie's family. Was Josh getting better? What did the doctors say? Was her mother getting any sleep? Did she need anything at the hospital? Did Hallie and her father have enough to eat?

There were several women riding in the passenger cabin with Mrs. Gladding. They were all island people, and they all had kind questions that Hallie had to answer patiently. They weren't gossips, Hallie knew. This was the way things worked on the island; when anyone was in trouble, everyone knew about it, and everyone paid attention. She had known these women all her life. They cared about Hallie and her family. It was wrong to resent their concern.

But just for once, Hallie wished they would leave her alone. Just this once, she wished that everybody didn't know all about everything that happened to everyone on Garnet Island, that everybody didn't *care* so much. Why couldn't they leave her alone, so she could talk to Melae?

The small passenger cabin was stuffy and airless, its salt-stained windows set too high in the steel walls for Hallie to see the harbor from where she sat. Mrs. Gladding kept glancing sympathetically at Hallie's scratched, filthy feet in the big flip-flops. Hallie's cheeks flamed as she realized that the minister's wife probably thought Hallie was wearing them because her father wasn't taking proper care of her. Hallie slid her feet back, trying to hide them under the bench. She felt as if she couldn't breathe. She couldn't see the water, couldn't see the whales. She wanted to get outside. She wanted to talk to Melae!

And besides, the kinder the women's questions, the gentler their comforting touches on Hallie's arm, the more she was afraid she might begin to cry. They were so gentle, so attentive—kinder than anyone but Melae had been to Hallie since Josh got hurt. She didn't want to cry in front of them, but a treacherous lump was growing in her throat.

"Well, you just let me know if you need anything, all right? Anything at all," said Mrs. Gladding, and let Hallie go at last with a final, friendly pat on the hand. But by the time Hallie had escaped from the stuffy passenger cabin into the fresh wind of the landing, the car ferry had steamed halfway across the harbor. The shipyard, and the whales, lay far behind.

Hallie squinted back over the sparkling harbor, but

through the glare of sun on water, she could see no sign of the whales. Most of the boats were gone—she could see that much. Only a few sailboats and motorboats still cruised near the shipyard.

Before she could try again to speak with Melae, the wheelhouse door swung open and Ira came out, grinning at Hallie as he trotted down the steps. Mack spoke from inside the wheelhouse.

"Hey, Hallie. Thought you might like to know, the harbor police drove off all those boats you were so worked up about. They've been on the radio, telling everybody on the harbor that it's a violation of federal law to get too close to those whales. Looks as if you can stop worrying now."

Hallie nodded and tried to smile. "Thanks, Mack."

The captain nodded and pushed the wheelhouse door shut again. Alone at last, Hallie closed her eyes. "Melae, can you hear me?" she whispered. "Are you still there?"

For a moment, there was no answer. But then Melae's voice came flowing powerfully through Hallie's body and soul.

I AM HERE, SMALL ONE.

Hallie opened her eyes in glad relief. But the whale had spoken slowly, her voice dragging a little, as if she was exhausted.

"Melae, are you all right?" Hallie asked worriedly.

The silence rushed with that seashell sound for a moment before the whale spoke. *I AM TIRED, SMALL ONE. PERHAPS IT WOULD BE BEST IF YOU AND I SPEAK LATER. THIS SPEAKING IS NOT EASY WORK, AND GLOBO NEEDS ME NOW.*

"Oh. Okay. Of course." Hallie tried not to feel hurt. She had not realized that it was hard for Melae to talk to her. And of course the whales needed rest after that morning's ordeal.

"But, Melae," she went on quickly. "I do need to tell you one thing. It's very important. Watch out for the shells, if they come back, okay? The people ... the legged ones, I mean, in the shells ... they might try to split you up, to chase you away from Globo."

BUT YOU MUST NOT LET THEM DO THAT, SMALL ONE, said Melae. *GLOBO IS NOT READY YET TO SWIM WITHOUT ME.*

"But I can't stop them, Melae. I'm just a kid. They won't listen to me."

OF COURSE THEY WILL LISTEN, said the whale. *YOU MUST SING TO THEM STRONGLY.*

"No, Melae, you don't understand," cried Hallie. "It doesn't work that way!"

TELL THEM, SMALL ONE, insisted the whale, her slow speech growing fainter. *YOU MUST TELL THEM. WE ARE TIRED. TELL THEM TO LEAVE US ALONE.*

Hallie sighed. "Okay, Melae," she said finally. "I'll try."

THANK YOU, SMALL ONE. NOW GLOBO AND I MUST REST, said Melae. *UNTIL LATER, THEN.*

"Okay, Melae. Bye," whispered Hallie. As the whale's presence ebbed away, she couldn't stop tears from filling her eyes. She had gone to the whale for help, but instead, the whale had asked for help from her. Melae trusted Hallie to help, she really believed that Hallie could keep people from chasing her away.

But, Hallie thought bitterly, what can I do? I'm the one who couldn't even help my own little brother when he needed me.

Feeling more alone than ever, Hallie stared back over the harbor, at the city falling away behind the ferry. The hospital's great bulk rose above the other buildings, its windows catching the sun in cold glints of white light. It was hard to believe that Josh and her mother were in there, and not back home on the island where they belonged. The lump that had begun to grow in her throat when Mrs. Gladding was talking to her was swelling again.

If only I could at least see Josh, she thought. It's so stupid. I can talk to a whale, but I can't even see my own little brother.

But even if I could, she thought then, what good would it do? Maybe Mom's right, and there's nothing I can do. I can't help Josh. I can't help the whales. And there's nobody at all to help me.

When the ferry docked at last at Garnet, Hallie stumbled down the stairs in the loose flip-flops, feeling so miserable that she hardly noticed when Ira called after her, "Don't lose my shoes in a puddle, now."

Even Ira thinks I'm weird, she thought gloomily as she flapped up the hill from the ferry landing. He said so. How much worse could things get?

Then somebody called her name, and she glanced up. Standing on the grocery store steps, frowning at Hallie, was Melissa.

10

Hallie blinked unhappily at her friend. "Hi."

"Hi." Without smiling, Melissa came down the steps with a bag of groceries in her arms and caught up with Hallie. The two girls walked along Ocean Avenue toward Melissa's house in silence.

"Those flip-flops aren't yours, are they?" asked Melissa finally. "They look kind of big."

"They're Ira's," answered Hallie. "He lent them to me, because I was in my bare feet."

Melissa glanced away. In a muffled voice, she asked, "Hallie, is that what you went rushing off to town for? To see Ira?"

"Of course not. What would I do that for?" Hallie stopped walking to stare at her friend.

"I don't know," said Melissa unhappily. "But I saw him wave at you when you got off the boat."

"Well, we did talk a little," admitted Hallie. "But it was only because I didn't have my shoes. I didn't even know Ira was working this boat, Melissa. That wasn't why I went off without you. I wouldn't do that."

Melissa gave Hallie a small, relieved smile. "I didn't really think that was it. I guess I only asked because it kind of hurt my feelings, when you ran off this morning. But then, why *did* you go to town, Hallie?"

Hallie bit her lip. She felt too tired and troubled to think of an excuse for her sudden trip to town. She didn't feel ready to try to tell Melissa the truth about Melae. Hallie wasn't entirely sure she believed herself that she could talk to a whale. Why would Melissa believe it? And, anyway, her friendship with the whale was secret, wonderful, and private, not to be shared—at least, not yet.

"I just had something to do," she said finally.

"Well, what?" Melissa was still smiling.

"Just something. I . . . I had to run an errand for my dad." Hallie watched her own scratched, dusty feet flapping along in Ira's big flip-flops.

The smile was slowly fading from Melissa's face. "I don't understand this, Hallie. You won't tell me anything. And you've been acting weird ever since yesterday. What's going on?"

Hallie tried to think of something to say, shrugged helplessly, and said nothing. Melissa stared at her for a moment, her chin quivering. Then, abruptly, she took off up the road, her dark hair bouncing on her shoulders, running awkwardly with her arms around the heavy grocery bag.

"Melissa, wait!" Hallie tried to run after her friend, but the flip-flops slowed her down. By the time she stopped to yank them off her feet, Melissa had already turned off the road onto the path to her house and disappeared among the trees.

Hallie ran, breathless, into the Gianopouloses' yard, but the front yard and the porch were empty. Melissa's house was an old Victorian summer cottage like Hallie's, but its paint was peeling and the gingerbread trim was broken off the porch. Where Hallie's yard bloomed with her mother's carefully tended flowers, Melissa's had bare patches where the grass had been worn away by the busy feet of Melissa's brothers and sisters. Surrounding the house was a cheerful, untidy jumble of toys and bicycles and lobster traps.

Ducking under a clothesline hung with diapers in the side yard, Hallie went around the house to look for Melissa in the back. She wasn't there, but her little brother Timmy was, making loud engine noises as he drove a toy truck through the dirt at the edge of the vegetable garden.

"Hi, Timmy. Have you seen Melissa?" asked Hallie.

"Hi, Hallie. Nope," said Timmy, and went back to his engine sounds.

Sighing, Hallie climbed the back steps and tapped on the kitchen door. When nobody came to the door, she pushed it open and stepped past some bushel baskets full of tomatoes into the kitchen.

It was obvious why nobody had answered her knock. After the quiet of the yard, the kitchen was startlingly noisy. Two of Melissa's younger sisters were arguing over a doll, the baby was crying, and Lobster, the Gianopouloses' big red-and-white dog, galloped through the confusion to jump up on Hallie, barking a joyful greeting. In the middle of it all, Mrs. Gianopoulos, her black hair slipping out of its knot, cradled the wailing baby on her hip while pouring juice for three-year-old Anthony.

"Lobster, get down! Celia, give Cynthia her doll, please. Hello, Hallie, dear. Did you have a good rest?" Mrs. Gianopoulos's calm smile lit her worn face as she set down the juice pitcher. Mrs. Gianopoulos was heavier than Hallie's mother, and she always looked tired, but with her dark eyes and hair like Melissa's, her serene smile and her gentle voice, Hallie thought she was beautiful.

"Um, yes, sure," Hallie said. "Um, how's your hand, Mrs. Gianopoulos?"

Mrs. Gianopoulos glanced down at the gauze bandage wrapped around her right hand. "Much better, honey. It isn't even sore today. Thanks for asking, and I don't want you worrying about it anymore. It wasn't really much of a burn, you know."

Hallie nodded dumbly. Mrs. Gianopoulos had burned herself when Josh got hurt, when she had grabbed him as he ran across the yard and pulled his burning pants off his legs. All that time, Hallie herself had stood unmoving at the edge of the yard, as frozen as a statue. She winced and looked away from the bandage on Mrs. Gianopoulos's plump brown hand.

The grocery bag Melissa had been carrying stood on the counter, but Melissa was not in the kitchen. The baby was crying harder now, and Hallie lifted her out of Mrs. Gianopoulos's arms. "There, there, Sophia, hush now," Hallie told the dark-eyed, red-faced baby, jiggling her up and down. "Mrs. Gianopoulos, did Melissa come in?"

"Yes, just a minute ago. She went up to the bathroom, I think. She should be right down," Mrs. Gianopoulos said.

But while Hallie danced the whimpering baby around the kitchen, and Mrs. Gianopoulos unpacked the groceries and sent the other children and the dog outside, Melissa didn't appear. Mrs. Gianopoulos glanced up the stairs with a small frown as she put the last of the food away, but all she said was, "Have you eaten yet, Hallie?"

"Well, I had a banana for breakfast. But that was a while ago," answered Hallie, her stomach growling. In fact, she was so hungry that she was having trouble preventing herself from snatching a tomato from the baskets by the back door and gobbling it whole.

"Well, it's almost lunchtime. I guess I'll make us something."

"Don't you want me to do it? I mean, doesn't it hurt your hand to cook?" asked Hallie.

"No, no. I told you, it isn't sore anymore. And, anyway, it's a big help for you to hold Sophia."

The baby stopped fussing at last and burrowed into Hallie's shoulder, sucking loudly on her fingers. Hallie sat down with her in the rocker while Mrs. Gianopoulos moved around the kitchen, slicing up a loaf of brown bread, some cheese, and a fat red tomato.

Except for the yelling of the children outside, the small sounds of the baby's sucking, and Mrs. Gianopoulos's knife on the cutting board, the kitchen was quiet. As Hallie rocked the baby, watching Mrs. Gianopoulos, her eyes suddenly filled with tears. For a moment, instead of Mrs. Gianopoulos quietly slicing the tomato into perfect ruby rounds, Hallie saw her own mother, thin and quick and always talking, sawing it into a juicy mess.

She closed her eyes and dropped her cheek onto Sophia's silky black curls. The baby's milky smell, the children's distant voices in the yard, Mrs. Gianopoulos setting plates on the table and pouring out glasses of juice . . . Melissa's house was so familiar and comforting, so safe, that it was like a second home.

But its very familiarity made Hallie feel the awful strangeness of what had happened to her life with a new sharpness. She wanted Melissa not to be angry with her. She wanted her own home. She wanted her father, she wanted her mother, she wanted Josh. Most of all, she wanted everything to be the way it used to be. Hallie swallowed and squeezed her eyes shut against her tears.

The floorboards creaked, and a gentle hand descended onto Hallie's hair and stroked it. She kept her eyes shut as a tear slid down her cheek, afraid that if she had to answer any questions, she would sob out loud.

But Mrs. Gianopoulos seemed to understand without being told that Hallie didn't want to talk. Still patting Hallie's hair with her bandaged hand, she said quietly, "Give me the baby now, dear, and eat your sandwich. After lunch, I'm going to can these tomatoes. Think you could give me a hand?"

Hallie nodded, her eyes still closed. Mrs. Gianopoulos took Sophia and turned away from Hallie to call the others. The children banged back into the kitchen, shouting about the worms they had dug in the garden, Lobster barking happily in their midst. With nobody paying attention to her, Hallie had a chance to swallow hard and force back her tears.

Melissa didn't show up for lunch, and Hallie didn't dare go upstairs to look for her. By the time Melissa came into the kitchen at last, Hallie was helping Celia and Cynthia cut the stems off the tomatoes while Mrs. Gianopoulos sterilized the canning jars. The baby was asleep in her crib in the corner, oblivious to the noise in the kitchen. Canning jars rattled in the boiling kettle, Celia and Cynthia sang along with the radio, and Anthony and Timmy growled as they drove their trucks over the kitchen floor. Nobody seemed to notice that Melissa barely glanced at Hallie. She didn't speak as she picked up a paring knife and set to work at the other end of the counter, as far away from Hallie as she could get.

But there was so much confusion in the kitchen that even calm Mrs. Gianopoulos lost patience at last. "Good Lord, in all this racket, I can't remember which jars I've sterilized and which ones I haven't. Hallie, Melissa, take the little ones outside so I can hear myself think, would you, please? Celia and Cynthia can finish up these tomatoes with me."

Hallie and Melissa's eyes met, reluctantly. Then the girls glanced away from each other again. Hallie put down her knife and followed while Melissa shooed Timmy and Anthony ahead of her out the back door.

Outside, Timmy trotted toward the road, yelling, "Let's go down to the beach and catch crabs!" Without waiting for Hallie, Melissa and Anthony went with him. Hallie followed more slowly, past her house and onto the path that led to the steps down the bluff.

The tide was going out, and a rim of dampness lay along the edge of the curving crescent of sand at the foot of the bluff. Anthony and Timmy, with Melissa right behind, ran out over the stony causeway that ended at Whaleback Rock. Hallie followed slowly, slipping in her big flip-flops on the loose piles of beachstones on the causeway. The stones chinked and rattled, and fragile blue mussel shells and whitened clamshells crunched under Hallie's rubber soles.

At the end of the point, Timothy and Anthony scrambled over the great boulders that lay tumbled on each other like a giant's building blocks, granite and quartz and rocks with no names that Hallie knew. In the crevices between the boulders were heaps of small brown periwinkle snails, tattered rags of seaweed, empty crab shells dropped by gulls, shards of broken glass, scraps of nylon rope. The surf boomed and broke over the rocks, glinting in the sunlight. But in the shelter of the great, gray bulk of Whaleback Rock, the waves broke more gently, whispering around boulders draped with mats of rockweed like hairy heads. Anthony and Timmy scrambled down among them to search for crabs under the clumps of weed.

"Careful, you guys." Melissa stood above them on top of Whaleback Rock, her back turned to Hallie. Hallie sat down on a boulder at the edge of the surf, wishing she could talk to Melissa, but uncertain what to say. Being able to talk to a whale had seemed like the most amazing and wonderful thing that had ever happened to Hallie. But was it really such a good thing, if it meant that she could no longer talk to her best friend?

Mr. Gianopoulos's red-and-white lobster boat bobbed in the distance on the glinting channel, and the creak of his winch as he hauled up a trap floated clearly across the water. Timmy and Anthony crowed with delight as they fished one small crab after another out from under the clumps of weed, scuttling on all fours over the rocks as easily as if they were crabs themselves.

Watching them, Hallie couldn't help thinking of Josh, who had always loved to fill a bucket full of crabs and watch them scrabbling at the sides of the pail with their small green claws. He never kept them more than a few minutes before he began to feel sorry for them. He'd put them all carefully back into their hiding places under the rockweed, and then happily catch himself a fresh bucketful. Josh had often spent a whole summer afternoon catching crabs and letting them go again. How long would it be, Hallie wondered, before he could spend an afternoon catching crabs again?

Beach pebbles sighed and tumbled as a wave lapped around her feet, cold as ginger ale. As the wave licked icily at her toes, exposed in Ira's flip-flops, Hallie thought for a moment that along with Timmy and Anthony's giggles, the boom of the surf, and the mewing of the gulls, she heard something else, a glad, distant piping. Could it be Melae, whistling?

As the surf sucked away, the sound disappeared, but when the next wave washed over her feet, she heard it again, and this time she knew that it was Melae. The whale didn't sound tired anymore. She was whistling joyously, that same giddy piping that she had called the glad song the day before. Melae's exuberant whistling echoed

135

up through the bones of Hallie's feet and spread through her, as warm and glad as happiness itself.

Hallie glanced quickly at the others. Could anyone else hear Melae? But none of the others was near the water. Timmy and Anthony squatted above the tide line, their dark heads close together as they examined a crab. Melissa sat on Whaleback Rock with her arms wrapped around her knees and her face turned coolly away from Hallie.

The water receded, and with it went Melae's whistling. The sun warmed Hallie's feet until the next icy wave washed in again, bringing with it Melae's voice. Again and again, as the waves rose and fell, the whale's music filled Hallie and ebbed away again, rising and falling with the muffled boom of the surf and the whispering hiss of the foam sucking through the pebbles.

This time, Hallie didn't try to speak to Melae; for now, she felt content just to listen. The song was even gladder than it had been the day before. Globo must be getting well, thought Hallie, if Melae can sing like that.

Behind Hallie, shells crunched under somebody's feet. She turned to see Timmy crouching among the rocks, his thatch of dark hair falling over his small, tanned face as he pried a periwinkle loose from a crevice. He turned the tiny brown snail over, studied it for a moment, and brought it up to his mouth.

Hallie watched in horrified fascination. Was he going to eat it? Holding it in his grubby fingers just in front of his mouth, Timmy pursed his lips and began, of all things, to hum at the snail in a loud, whining drone.

Hallie couldn't watch in silence any longer. "What in the world are you doing?" she demanded.

Timmy stopped humming. "Singing to this snail," he answered matter-of-factly.

"*Singing* to it?"

"Yup. Come see."

Hallie scrambled over the weed-slicked rocks to Timmy, crouched down beside him, and peered at the tiny brown creature clutched in his dirty hands. He was humming again, in a tuneless drone, like a bagpipe.

"See? He likes it."

Inside the curved shelter of its tiny shell, the slick brown surface of the snail's foot was tilting open, like a door. From behind it peeped two small, gleaming brown protuberances, reaching tentatively out of the shell toward Timmy's mouth.

"He's peeking out, see? He's listening," said Timmy. As if startled by his speech, the periwinkle vanished promptly back into its shell, its foot sliding tightly back into place.

Hallie was astonished. "Can I try that?"

"Sure." Timmy handed her the periwinkle. Feeling a little ridiculous, she brought the tiny creature up to her face and hummed at it the way Timmy had.

Sure enough, as she droned, the foot tipped open again. The two protuberances reached out slowly, questioning, curious, toward Hallie's humming. Were they the snail's eyes, or ears, or something else altogether? Hallie had no idea. The protuberances wiggled a little, as if signaling something. She giggled involuntarily, and the periwinkle retreated as abruptly as before, its smooth brown foot sliding over the opening with an almost audible click, like the closing of a door.

Hallie was enchanted. "I never knew you could sing to snails."

"Oh, I always knew about *that*," Timmy bragged. She grinned at him as he scuttled away over the rocks, letting out a yip of delight as he found another crab under a clump of weed.

Gently, Hallie set the periwinkle back into its crevice in the rock. She felt as unreasonably happy as if she had been given a present. Everything sings, she thought. Everything listens. Birds, people, the wind—everything makes some kind of music. A person can even sing to a snail.

She looked up to find Melissa looking down at her with a small smile. "I don't believe you didn't know about humming to snails," Melissa said. "Everybody knows about that." Her smile was wary, but hopeful, as if Timmy and his snail had somehow begun to heal the rift between them.

Hallie smiled back at her. Melissa's smile was so familiar, so welcome, that all of a sudden it seemed ridiculous to be distant from her. "Everybody but me, I guess. Listen, Melissa, I'm really sorry about this morning. I didn't mean to hurt your feelings. I guess I've had a lot on my mind lately."

Melissa slid down the side of the rock to stand closer to Hallie. "I know you have," she said sympathetically. "It's because of Josh, right?"

"Partly," admitted Hallie. "But there's something else,

too. It's those whales. You know, the two pilot whales in the harbor that we saw on the ferry yesterday? I've been really worried about them."

"The whales?" Melissa looked startled. "It didn't seem like you even noticed them yesterday."

"I did, though," said Hallie. "I'm afraid the sick one's going to die. I took the ferry this morning to look at them and see if they were okay."

"But I don't get it. Why couldn't you tell me about that?"

"I don't know. I guess I was afraid you would think it was stupid or . . . or something." Hallie hesitated, studying her friend's small face, her friendly dark eyes, her serious mouth. Why shouldn't she tell Melissa about Melae? Melissa was Hallie's oldest friend. She'd understand, wouldn't she? Of course she would. And suddenly, Hallie knew exactly how she wanted to introduce Melae to her friend.

"Melissa, come into the water with me, would you, please?" Hallie said.

"Into the water?" asked Melissa. "You're kidding, right? It's freezing in there."

"I know. But come wading with me, anyway, okay? Just for a minute."

"Well, okay, I guess," said Melissa doubtfully. "But this had better be good."

"It is, it is." Hallie waited while Melissa pulled off her sneakers and stuffed her socks inside them. Then she took her friend's hand and tugged her toward the shallow surf washing around the rocks. This was the right way—not to say anything until after Melissa had listened to Melae's strange, exuberant whistling, like nothing else on earth. Then Melissa would know.

And what if Melissa couldn't hear Melae? Hallie pushed the small, doubtful question away into the back of her mind. Of course Melissa would hear the whale, and then she'd understand everything.

Hallie waded into the shallow water, ignoring the shock of cold around her ankles, and Melissa followed reluctantly, shivering as a wave washed over her bare feet. "Ouch! It's freezing in here."

"I know," said Hallie. "But be quiet and listen for a minute, anyway."

Holding Melissa's hand, she closed her eyes, lifted her face to the sky, stood still and listened. But as the cold waves rushed over Hallie's tingling feet, she heard only the wash of surf on rocks and the small voices of Timmy and Anthony mingling with the wails of the gulls. Melae's glad whistling had disappeared. Hallie stood still, straining to listen, but there was nothing to hear. While Hallie had been out of the water, humming to the periwinkle with Timmy, the whale had stopped whistling.

Why? A little troubled, Hallie squinted out over the water. "Melae?" she whispered tentatively.

No answer came from the whale, but Melissa asked, "What?"

Melissa had thought that Hallie was talking to her, she realized. "Nothing, nothing," Hallie said quickly, still listening to the odd silence beneath the roar of the surf. Why had Melae stopped singing?

But Melissa's hand was warm in hers, and just then, the

relief of being close again to her friend felt more important than wondering about the whale. I'll tell Melissa later, thought Hallie, when Melae starts singing again. She'll probably start whistling again any minute now.

Melissa turned to Hallie, her face perplexed. "What did you want me to listen to?" she said. "All I can hear is Dad's boat out there. It sounds like his engine needs work. Was that what you wanted me to hear?"

"Um, no. I just . . . I just wanted you to hear the ocean noises," stammered Hallie. "Doesn't it all sound nice? Kind of like music?"

Around the girls, the surf boomed and hissed, and Timmy and Anthony chattered in their light, young voices. A flock of ducks flapped, quacking, down onto the water beyond the waves. Out on the channel, Mr. Gianopoulos's lobster boat chugged in its steady bass rhythm, and over the water floated the long, distant blare of the ferry horn.

Melissa was shivering. "Well, yes, I guess it sounds pretty, the way it always does. But what did we have to wade into this freezing water to listen to it for?"

Hallie shrugged, smiling at Melissa helplessly, hopefully. "Oh, just to make it more interesting, I guess," she said.

Melissa shook her head. "You really are getting weird, you know," she said, but she was smiling back at Hallie.

Maybe it doesn't matter, thought Hallie suddenly. Maybe Melissa and I can still be best friends, even if we can't always tell each other everything, even if she never does hear Melae. Hallie couldn't help smiling at the thought, and the smile became a laugh, bubbling up in her from Melae's whistling still echoing in her memory, from the snail, from the September sun on her shoulders, from the warmth of her friend's hand in hers.

Melissa was laughing now, too, as if Hallie had told her some wonderful joke. The two girls stood ankle-deep in the icy surf, holding hands, giggling like a pair of little children, until Melissa finally stopped long enough to gasp, "Can we get out of this freezing water now?"

"Okay, okay." Hallie let Melissa tug her back out of the surf. Still chuckling a little, out of breath from laughing, the two girls climbed up onto Whaleback Rock and sat together, their shoulders touching. They rubbed their cold feet and listened to the music of the surf and the wind and the voices of Melissa's two small brothers, calling good-bye to their crabs as they let them go, one by one, to scrabble back into their hiding places in the weed-thatched rocks.

11

Hallie didn't mention the whales to Melissa again that afternoon. She waded into the water and listened several times, but no whale whistling came piping through the waves.

At the end of the afternoon, she and Melissa and the wet, tired boys finally straggled back up to the house. Hallie could hear the phone ringing inside as they trooped up the back steps. Mrs. Gianopoulos met them at the door, holding out the cordless phone to Hallie.

"It's your father, for you," she said.

Hallie took the phone and carried it past the empty tomato baskets into the kitchen, where rows of gleaming, ruby red jars stood cooling on the counter. "Hello, Dad?"

"Hello, Hallie." The cordless phone crackled with static, and her father's voice sounded tinny and far away. "How are you, honey?"

"Okay, I guess." Hallie was thinking quickly. Maybe now she could ask her father about separating the whales. She had promised Melae to try to do something about it, after all. "Um, Dad, I'm glad you called. There's something I wanted to ask you . . ."

But her father's voice overrode hers. "Hallie, we need to talk about this evening."

Hallie stopped short. "Is something wrong?"

"No, no. The thing is, Hallie, I'm going to stay here at the hospital with Josh tonight. Your mother is worn out. I finally talked her into going over to your aunt Rose's to sleep. I don't want you at home alone. I was calling to see if you can stay with the Gianopouloses tonight."

"Well, okay, I guess," said Hallie, a little reluctantly. She had wanted to go back down to the beach that night, to listen for Melae again. That would be hard to do at the Gianopouloses'.

Her father sounded a little rushed. "I'll be home sometime tomorrow, okay? Let me talk to Thea now, so I can make sure it's all right for you to stay."

"Um, Dad, wait," said Hallie. "I wanted to ask you something."

"Well, make it quick, please, sweetheart. Josh's doctor just came in, and I need to talk to her," said her father.

"It's about those whales."

"Well, what about them?"

"Well . . . um . . ." Hallie floundered. How could she ask her father about separating the whales without letting him know that she had overheard him that morning? "I was wondering what's going to happen now. What are you planning to do about them?"

"I'm not planning anything, Hallie." Her father's voice was hard to hear through the static in the phone. "I've been thinking about Josh and your mother this afternoon, not about whales. It's out of my hands now,

144

anyway. A team from the aquarium came into town today, and they'll handle it from here on in."

"Oh. Well, do you know what they're going to do?"

"No, I really don't," her father said. "Hallie, the doctor doesn't have much time. Let me talk to Thea now, please."

"Dad, I'll tell her," said Hallie quickly. "It'll be all right for me to stay here. It always is."

"Well, if you think so." Her father sounded relieved. She heard him call away from the receiver, "Dr. Abbott, I'll be there in one minute. Sorry to keep you waiting. Hallie, tell Thea and Nick I'll be home tomorrow around noon, all right? And thank them for me."

"I will, Dad."

"See you tomorrow then. I love you." Hallie could barely hear her father through the noise on the line.

"I love you, too, Dad. Bye." Hallie hung up.

Melissa and Timmy were setting the table for dinner, and their mother was stirring a fragrant pot of tomato sauce on the stove. The rising steam curled the wisps of black hair around Mrs. Gianopoulos's face. "How is your father?" she asked Hallie.

Hallie didn't know she was going to lie until she opened her mouth. "He's fine. He'll be home later on," she told Mrs. Gianopoulos, almost as startled by her own words as if someone else had spoken. "He's coming home on the seven-thirty boat. He wants me to meet him at home."

"Well, you can stay and have dinner with us first, then. It'll be good to have some help eating all this spaghetti," Mrs. Gianopoulos said, with her warm, tired smile. "And I'll send a plate with you for your father, when he gets home tonight."

"Thanks." Hallie nodded, not meeting her eyes. She glanced out the window, where the ocean glinted through the birches that rimmed the backyard. She didn't like lying to Mrs. Gianopoulos, but she wanted to talk to Melae tonight. It would be impossible to slip out of the crowded house, away from Mrs. Gianopoulos's watchful eyes, without somebody asking where she was going. But at home, all by herself, it would be easy.

As Hallie picked up a handful of forks to help set the table, an old, black pickup truck rattled to a stop outside the kitchen door.

"Daddy!" As Melissa's father stepped into the kitchen, Timmy and Anthony ran to him and wrapped their arms around his legs.

"Hi, guys!" Beaming down at them, Mr. Gianopoulos patted their heads with his wide, square hands, stained and dirty from his day on the lobster boat. He was short and dark, and his rich bass voice was the backbone of the choir at the island church. He sang when he was lobstering; people on shore sometimes heard bass hymns come rolling in with the waves. But when he was angry, that same deep voice could boom out almost as loudly as the ferry horn. When she was younger, Hallie had been a little afraid of him before she learned that all Mr. Gianopoulos ever did was yell, and that when the yelling was over, his anger was gone, too, blasted away like a storm blown out to sea.

He crossed the kitchen to the stove, where Mrs.

Gianopoulos put down her spoon and hugged her husband as gladly as the boys had, ignoring the tang of diesel fuel and lobster bait on his fishing coveralls.

At the dinner table, Sophia crowed and banged on her high chair tray while the rest of the family all talked at once, passing around huge bowls of spaghetti and salad. They hardly ever ate lobster; Mr. Gianopoulos caught so much that they were all tired of it. Hallie's family ate more seafood than the Gianopouloses ever did.

It was good spaghetti, though, rich and filling, seasoned with the fresh basil that Mrs. Gianopoulos grew beside the tomatoes. Hungry from the long afternoon on the beach, Hallie ate a large plateful, sitting between Melissa and Timmy, trying to keep up with several conversations at once. But when Mr. Gianopoulos's big voice boomed out, everybody stopped talking and listened.

"I saw one of those pothead whales today, heading out to sea."

Hallie's fork stopped in midair. She stared at Melissa's father, unable to speak.

"What happened to the other one, Nick?" asked Mrs. Gianopoulos.

Mr. Gianopoulos took a big bite of garlic bread and chewed it with agonizing slowness before he swallowed it and answered, "I don't know. I was out on the other side of the island this afternoon, not far off Apple Knob. A flock of boats came along, heading out from the city. Little boats, close together. One of them was the harbor police launch. Couldn't figure out what they were doing. When they got closer I saw they had one of those potheads in front of them. They kept going, heading down east, beyond Ruby Island, where I couldn't see them anymore. But it looked like they were heading that pothead out into open water, just like they tried to do the other day."

Hallie found her voice. "Are you sure there was only one whale?"

"I only saw one," Mr. Gianopoulos said. "It swam right past me."

"But what happened to the other one?"

He shrugged. "I didn't see any sign of it."

Had Globo beached himself? Or died? Melissa was trying to catch Hallie's eye, but Hallie hardly noticed. She was swallowing her mouthful of spaghetti as if it were sawdust. It must have been Melae that Mr. Gianopoulos had seen; that was why she had stopped singing. The rescue team had separated the whales and chased Melae out of the harbor, just as her father had predicted. Hallie had never thought that this would happen so soon. She hadn't done anything to stop it. She had let Melae down. She had failed.

The rest of the meal seemed to last forever. Usually Hallie was eager for Mrs. Gianopoulos's rich desserts, but tonight she didn't want any apple pie. It was Celia's night to clear the table, and when at last she reached past Hallie to take away her untouched plate, Hallie jumped up from the table. "Mrs. Gianopoulos, before I go home, can I turn on the evening news?" she asked.

Melissa's mother nodded, and Melissa and Hallie hurried into the living room together to switch on the set.

The newscast was already in progress. The girls sat impatiently through a report on a strike at one of the fish-cutting factories, and then the same auburn-haired announcer Hallie had seen the night before appeared. "A rescue team from the National Aquarium tried to save the female pilot whale who has been keeping a sick whale company in the harbor today, by driving her out to sea. A representative said that the effort had succeeded, and the whale was last seen swimming northeast. The female whale made no attempt to return to the harbor, and the social bond keeping her with the ailing whale appeared to be broken. The key to her survival, the experts said, will be whether she can locate and rejoin a group of other pilot whales. As of this evening, the remaining whale is still alive, and swimming in the harbor."

Watching, Hallie breathed a sharp sigh of relief. At least Globo hadn't died or beached himself. And Melae couldn't have gone far without him. The announcer was still talking. "According to the aquarium experts, if the ailing whale is still in the harbor tomorrow morning, an attempt may be made to capture him for medical treatment. And now this, from Channel Nine News." The announcer smiled brilliantly as her face was replaced by a commercial for bathroom cleaner.

Hallie switched off the television and stood staring at the blank screen. It was true; the whales had been split up, and Melae was gone. I have to go down to the beach, she thought urgently. I have to talk to Melae. Right now.

"I've got to go home now," she said out loud.

"I'll come with you," offered Melissa, but before Hallie could decide how to answer, Mr. Gianopoulos called from the kitchen. "Not tonight, Melissa. I need help with these dishes."

"Oh, Dad!" protested Melissa.

But her father was adamant. "You girls have had plenty of time together today. Come on in here now, honey. I'll wash, you dry."

"Can I help?" offered Hallie to be polite, as Melissa went reluctantly into the kitchen.

She was relieved when Mrs. Gianopoulos said, "No, no, run along, Hallie. The boat will be in soon, and your father wants you at home. Here, take him this." She handed Hallie a warm plate covered tightly with aluminum foil.

Hallie took the plate guiltily. "Okay, thanks. And thanks for my dinner, too. Good night, Mr. and Mrs. Gianopoulos. See you tomorrow, Melissa." Melissa waved a dishcloth at her with a grimace as Hallie carried the plate out the door.

The evening was cool and still. Hallie ran across the Gianopouloses' yard and down the road, past cottages whose lit windows glowed golden in the gathering twilight, to her own house, dark and silent in its empty yard. She stopped there only long enough to set the covered plate of spaghetti down in the grass behind her mother's asters. As she straightened up, she remembered her clothes still hidden behind the lilac bush. I'd better remember to pick these things up before the next time I mow the lawn, she thought.

Crickets sang as Hallie ran down the steps to the beach, and the perfume of wild roses hung heavy in the darkening air. The tide had gone out, and the beach spread empty and damp. The boom of the surf was muffled. The rank, marshy smell of low tide rose from the cove, and gulls stalked across the exposed seabed on their thin legs, hunting snails.

Hallie pulled off Ira's flip-flops, tossed them onto the sand, and ran down to the waterline. The tide was so low that she had to go halfway across the cove before she reached the water.

She splashed finally into the shallows, calling as soon as her feet touched the water.

"Melae! Hey, Melae! Can you hear me?"

She stood still and listened. She could hear the soft slapping of waves against the sand. A trawler chugged past the mouth of the cove, and a bell buoy clanged in the distance. But Melae said nothing.

Hallie called again. "Melae? Melae!"

But there was no answer.

"Globo?" she tried after a while. "Globo? Can you hear me?"

But the other whale had never answered her before, and tonight was no different. In the dim light, a cormorant bobbed on the water, its long, black neck like a narrow question mark against the silvery sea. As Hallie stood still, listening for the whale, the cormorant suddenly ducked under the water and disappeared.

"Melae!" called Hallie again. "Where did you go? Why don't you answer me?"

Nobody answered. The evening breeze bit, damp and chilly, through Hallie's sweater. As suddenly as a magic trick, the cormorant reappeared, far from the spot where it had vanished, bobbing calmly on the water as though nothing had happened. Hallie stood alone in the cold water, hugging Melissa's sweater around herself, listening. But there was nothing to hear.

12

"Hal-leeeee! Hal-leeeee!"

In her dark bedroom, Hallie sat up, half asleep. The far-off cry pierced the night again, trailing away in a thin, desperate wail.

"Hal-leeeee!"

"Josh? Joshie? What's the matter?" As her own sleep-furred voice brought Hallie awake, she remembered that Josh couldn't be calling her. He wasn't home, and neither were her parents. She had come in from the beach to an empty house and gone to bed alone.

But the strange, panicked cry still echoed in her ears. What had she heard?

She sat still, listening. A breeze rustled the curtain at her open window, carrying the ordinary sounds of the island night—the barking of someone's wakeful dog; the constant, gentle booming of surf; the distant clang of a bell buoy; the faraway throbbing of the city, still humming with life even in the middle of the night. Nobody called her name.

It must have been a dream, she thought finally. She didn't remember dreaming, though. And there had been something so real about that shrill, scared sound. It had pulled her out of sleep as sharply as if it had yanked her by the hair. Her heart was still pounding from the shock of it. Hallie shook her head in the darkness and lay down again on her bunched-up pillow.

Her heartbeat had slowed almost to normal and her eyes were closing when she heard it again, slicing through the night.

"Hal-leeee! Hal-leeee!"

She was out of bed and running through the dark house before the cry had trailed away. The thready, desolate wail had come from outside, from the direction of the beach. In some small, clearheaded portion of her sleepy brain, she knew that whoever was calling her could not be Josh. But she grabbed a flashlight from a kitchen drawer and ran toward the lost sound, now fading on the wind, as urgently as if it was her brother's voice she heard. She felt she could not get there fast enough.

Outdoors, a full moon hung over the trees. Its pale light silvered the birches and sumacs, guiding Hallie's way across the yard, so that she didn't need to turn the flashlight on. Her long nightgown caught on a tangle of wild rose brambles as she ran onto the beach path. She tore it free and kept running.

The wail rose through the air again, closer and clearer. Now, she realized that she was not hearing her name, after all. Though it had the same two-noted rhythm as her name, the cry was a wordless squeal, rising from its first lower note to a high, trembling whistle.

Still, she was stumbling down the steps to the beach before she understood what she was hearing. In the cove, a large, black, solitary something broke the silvery surface of the water. It rolled and floundered, shedding drops of water that sparkled in the moonlight like diamonds.

Hallie froze on the bottom step. The dark shape heaved again in the moonlight. At first she thought it was Melae, but then, by his tall fin and scarred black skin, she recognized Globo, his body gleaming as he floundered in the shallow water. He was trapped in the cove, not far off the beach, stuck on a sandbar.

Globo's frightened whistles of distress were completely unlike Melae's deep, sweet voice, which Hallie had heard not with her ears but through her bones and her heart and her soul. Globo's squealing came only to her ears. It carried no message except the simple fact of the whale's panic and confusion.

The tide was high, and water lapped at the sand only a few feet from the bottom step. Hallie stepped down onto the thin margin of sand, staring out at the floundering animal, trying to think. As she watched, Globo heaved sideways and managed to roll free into deeper water on the far side of the sandbar. He stopped whistling and swam to the middle of the cove, where he began to circle anxiously.

Hallie could see Globo's bewilderment and fear almost as clearly as if he were speaking to her. Now, it was not boat engines that frightened him; it was the rocky shores around him and the cove bottom rising beneath him, hemming him in, baffling him.

He must have gotten into the cove through one of the gaps in the Barrier Rocks that Mr. Gianopoulos sometimes brought his lobster boat through, she thought. Maybe he had been heading out of the harbor toward the ocean, when the long arm of Whaleback Point misdirected him into the cove. However he had gotten in, he couldn't find his way out again now. But he had to get out soon. At high tide, the cove was deep enough for a lobster boat or a smallish whale like Globo, but once the tide went out, much of the cove bottom would be exposed. The water would be too shallow, and Globo would be trapped.

"Oh, Globo," whispered Hallie, her voice small and frightened. "Melae, help. Where are you?" Grabbing the hem of her nightgown up around her knees, she ran into the water, not even noticing the cold, shouting, "Melae! I need you! Globo needs you!"

But she knew before she called that Melae would not answer. "Melae!" she cried again, her voice rising in panic on the last note just like Globo's. But no answer came. Melae was gone, chased off into deep water somewhere, too far away to hear. If she were nearby, Melae would be here with Globo, after all. She wouldn't leave him trapped like this if she knew about it.

Hallie waded deeper into the water, closer to the heaving whale. "Globo!" she called, hoping that by some miracle, he would understand her now as Melae did. "Globo, turn around. Get out of the cove! You've got to swim away from here!"

But except for a sharp puff of breath from his blowhole each time he rose to the surface, Globo did not respond. He was not even whistling anymore.

What could she do? Hallie stood motionless, staring.

As she watched, Globo's black tail rose up into the moonlight and slammed down against the water with a resounding slap. Why had she thought that he was small? He was far bigger than she was. Even if she could swim well enough to get out into the deep water near him, trying to push him would be like trying to push an elephant. With that great black tail, he could swat her like a fly.

If her father were here, Hallie thought, he would know how to handle this. But he wasn't on the island, and even if Hallie ran to the phone and called the hospital, he couldn't come. There were no boats to Garnet in the middle of the night. And hadn't her mother said once that the hospital turned off the phones to the patients' rooms at night? Maybe she wouldn't be able to reach him at all. Anyway, there wasn't time to try. Hallie would have to figure out how to handle this without her father's help.

But she had to get help from somebody. She couldn't do anything alone, after all. She would wake up the Gianopouloses, and get the police, and everybody else she knew on the island, to help drive the whale out of the cove. Hallie turned to run for help, but as she did, Globo gave a heave and swam back toward the beach again.

"No, Globo, get away!" cried Hallie. Her eye fell on Mr. Gianopoulos's dinghy, tied to its mooring near her, half afloat on the high tide. She dropped the flashlight into the dinghy, yanked one of the oars free of its oar-lock, and ran into the water, yelling and slapping the surface with the oar over and over again, making as much noise as she could. Noise scared whales, she knew that much. Maybe she could make enough noise to turn Globo away from the beach. She could even hit him with the oar if she had to.

But she didn't have to hit him. Whether it was the commotion she made or not, she didn't know, but Globo circled raggedly away from the beach again and swam back out toward the mouth of the cove. Hallie watched, holding her breath. He was heading for the Barrier Rocks. Would he swim free on his own?

"Just a little farther, Globo," cried Hallie, clutching the oar. "You're so close. You're almost there!" But before he reached the rocks, Globo stopped as if he were suddenly exhausted and began to circle aimlessly again.

"Globo! Don't stop now!" Though she knew the whale couldn't understand her, Hallie couldn't help yelling. Her forgotten nightgown, soaked and heavy, clung to her legs as she splashed through the shallows to the dinghy. She dropped the oar into it and yanked with trembling fingers at the stiff, new rope, struggling to undo the tight knot, hardly aware herself of what she was doing. If she could just somehow lead Globo through the Barrier Rocks, he'd be in deep water again. Maybe then he'd be safe. At least, he'd be far enough away from shore to let her go for help. She couldn't leave now, when he was almost there.

With a last yank, she undid the knot and tugged the rope free of the steel eye anchored in the rock. Just as she had done once before, she shoved the dinghy out onto the water, wading along beside it. "I'm sorry, Mr. Gianopoulos," she whispered as the boat bobbed free and she swung herself into it. "I shouldn't take your boat, I know, but this is important. I won't lose it this time, I promise."

She grabbed up the free oar and used it to pole the boat around so that its bow pointed toward the whale. She wasn't sure just what she planned to do; she had a vague idea of rowing close to Globo and trying to get him to follow her, or of pounding on the water again with the oar, making all the noise she could, to chase him out. She knew only that she had to get close to the whale to help him in whatever way she could.

She settled herself on the plank seat, slid the oar pin back into the oarlock, and gathered up the oars. Watching Globo over her shoulder, she braced her feet against the planks of the boat bottom and dragged the oars through the water as powerfully as she could. She leaned over, putting her back into each stroke. It seemed a little easier than it had in the fog the morning before; maybe she had learned something. And this time, she could see where she was going by the pale light of the moon. The boat zigged and zagged, but with each stroke it slid across the water, away from the beach, closer and closer to the whale.

The black water looked bottomless under the dinghy, as if Hallie were rowing across a moonless sky. Phosphorescence trailed like stars away from her oars. She could feel the water yielding to the pull of her oars, and she was filled suddenly with a sense of power and hope as she and the dinghy moved over the water, toward the black body of the whale.

It only took her a few minutes to reach Globo. He

hung, exhausted, at the surface, breath escaping from his blowhole in short, explosive puffs. Hallie stopped rowing when she was still a little distance away, out of range of that big tail.

She lifted the dripping oars free of the water and set them down on the dinghy floor. The dinghy rocked gently on the choppy waves. She meant to shout, but when she spoke, her voice was soft and coaxing.

"Come on, Globo," she said. "Just swim a little farther. You can do it."

The whale let out a breath, and a small cloud of steam escaped from his blowhole, glinting faintly in the moonlight. He didn't move.

"Globo! Come on, you have to swim!" She tugged an oar free of the oarlock, heaved it into the air, and slapped it down onto the water, as close to him as she dared. "Globo! Swim!"

The black skin rippled slightly, like a horse shaking off a fly, but the whale still didn't move. He was even bigger than she had thought, his body longer than the dinghy. His fin rose high out of the water, reminding her uncomfortably of sharks.

She sat still a moment, staring at him, the feeling of hope beginning to ebb away. Maybe she should have gone straight for help. Maybe she had just wasted time, rowing out here. Why had she thought she could do anything to help? She was so small, and he was so big. It was just as her mother had said about Josh. There was nothing she could do.

But as she watched, Globo began to swim again toward the shore. Whatever she should have done before, it was too late to go for help now. She had to do whatever she could. She took a breath and yelled again, whacking the oar against the surface of the water. Globo let out a long breath like a sigh. Slowly, his back rose into an arc and the fin slid from view as he dove silently beneath the water.

Now where was he? Would he come up again under the dinghy, and spill her into the water? "Globo! Globo, where are you?" shouted Hallie.

She glanced back at the shoreline. Maybe somebody would hear her yelling and come to help. But the beach lay still and empty under the moon. The island was a humped, dark silhouette, no house lights glimmering among its shadowed trees. The houses near the water all belonged to summer people; they had closed them up and gone away. The only year-round house along the bluff was Hallie's own, and it, of course, was empty. She was as alone on the cove as she had been the morning she had fallen out of the dinghy. But at least then Melae had heard her and come to her rescue. Now there was nobody to hear.

There was a puff and a splash behind her, and Hallie glanced around to see that Globo had emerged again, a little closer to the gap in the rocks. "Hey! That's right! That's the way! Keep going!"

Trying to keep the dinghy between Globo and the shore, she slapped the oar against the water, drummed on the bottom of the boat with both of her bare feet, and yelled. But on the wide black water under the great bowl of the night sky, all the noise she was capable of making seemed very small. It had no impact on Globo. He dove again and reemerged, circling nearer to the dinghy this time, no closer to the gap in the Barrier Rocks.

It wasn't working. She'd never chase him out this way. How could she make more noise? Hallie glanced around in frustration. The dinghy was empty except for Hallie and the oars and the flashlight she had brought from home, rolling back and forth on the floorboards of the boat. Moonlight glinted on the dented housing of the old outboard motor clamped to the stern of the dinghy. The outboard! Hallie stared at it, a new idea forming in her mind.

Could she start the outboard? She never had before, and she wouldn't dare try to use it to move the dinghy; she had no idea how to control the powerful little engine. But Mr. Gianopoulos had left the outboard tipped out of the water, its propeller angled safely above the waves. If she started the motor like that, it wouldn't move the boat. But maybe, just maybe, it would make enough noise to drive Globo away from it and out of the cove.

Hallie swung the oars into the bottom of the boat and slid back to the stern, careful not to stand up or to rock the dinghy. If she fell in this time, Melae wouldn't be here to help her. By the moonlight, she examined the rust-speckled motor. It had a starting cord with a handle, just like Hallie's parents' lawn mower. She knew how to start the mower; you pulled on the cord. Maybe she could start the outboard the same way.

She gave the starting cord an experimental yank, but nothing happened. Her heart sank. Maybe it was out of gas. Or maybe it didn't even work. She had never seen Mr. Gianopoulos use it.

She leaned closer and peered at the little engine. By the dim light of the moon, she could see a control panel below the starting cord with switches and buttons. There was lettering above the switches, but the moonlight was too dim to read it.

Hallie fumbled in the bottom of the dinghy, found the flashlight, and flicked it on. To her surprise, it worked, shedding a wan, uncertain circle of light onto the dinghy floorboards.

Globo let out another puff, and she glanced at him. He was still swimming in his tight circle. "Stay there," she ordered him. "Keep away from the beach, do you hear me?"

Then she turned back to the outboard, directing the dim beam of light onto the control panel. There was a throttle with a turtle on the bottom and a rabbit at the top. Beside the throttle, a red button was marked STOP and below that, there was a black switch labeled POWER.

She dropped the flashlight, flicked the power switch on, grabbed the black plastic handle of the power cord, and yanked it out again. This time, the engine coughed reluctantly once and died away into silence. Encouraged, she yanked again and again, pulling the cord so hard that her shoulder ached. The cord was salt-stiffened and hard to pull, but the engine coughed, sputtered, and on the ninth or tenth yank, yowled suddenly to life.

She pushed the throttle all the way up to the rabbit, and the engine's roar seemed to split the night apart. Hallie jumped away from the screaming motor, watching the propeller blades spinning wildly in the moonlight. Her nose filled with fumes and her ears with the whining racket, and the whole dinghy vibrated.

But it was working! Beyond the dinghy, Globo's fin split the water. He was swimming away from the earsplitting roar of the motor, toward the rocks. "That's right! Keep going, Globo!" Hallie screamed, though she could hardly hear her own voice above the outboard.

But Globo stopped and began circling again before he reached the opening. Hallie grabbed up the oars and rowed after him, splashing water into the dinghy in her haste. As she got closer, bringing the noise of the outboard along with her, Globo slid beneath the surface again, and she held her breath. When he emerged again he was in one of the gaps between the stones, swimming for the open sea.

"Yahoo!" Hallie shook both fists up at the moon in victory. Then she took the oars again and rowed after the whale, the shrieking propeller still chopping at the air, until she and the dinghy were poised in the gap in the rocks where the sheltered water of the cove gave way to the waves of the open ocean.

Beyond the cascades of surf rising into the moonlight around the base of Whaleback Rock, Globo's sharp black fin broke the moonlit surface once and disappeared again. Hallie sculled gently with the oars, trying to keep the rocking dinghy from following the whale onto the rough water. Shaking her head against the noise, she pushed the stop button, and the shrieking engine abruptly died, leaving a ringing silence.

Globo's fin emerged once more, and the soft explosion of his breath, barely audible, floated across the water. He was much farther out this time, safely past Whaleback, past Garnet Island altogether, headed out to sea. He swam fast and strong, as powerfully as if he had never been sick.

"Keep going, Globo! Hooray!" shouted Hallie. He was well, he was out of the cove, he was free. She couldn't help bouncing on the dinghy seat in her glee, rocking the dinghy alarmingly. She clutched the gunwales and sat still, chuckling to herself.

"I did it, Melae," she whispered. "I did it, all by myself! I got him out!"

She gazed intently at the sea, straining to catch one more glimpse of that black fin, but all she could see now were the long pale stripes of combers rolling in toward shore under the moon. The quiet of the night was broken only by the splash of waves against the Barrier Rocks and the softer booming of the surf on the rocky shore. Out on the water, something glinted. Was it a spark of moonlight on a wave, or was it Globo's fin, catching the light once more before he disappeared?

She couldn't tell. "Good-bye, Globo. Good luck. Good-bye!" she whispered into the great silence of the night. Then she picked up her oars again and began the lonely row back over the dark water to the land.

13

After she had pulled the dinghy up onto the damp sand and tied it securely back where it belonged, Hallie found that she could not go back home to bed. Excitement still fizzed through her veins like ginger ale. She wanted to dance down the beach and leap through the moonlight. She wanted to sing at the top of her voice. She wanted to wake Melissa up and tell her all about what she had done.

But what she did do, at last, was to run along the edge of the cove, over the causeway, all the way out to the end of the point. She climbed onto the cool, pitted top of Whaleback Rock, damp with spray, and stood on its highest ridge, gazing out over the breakers at the moonlit sea beyond. She could see no sign of Globo.

There was always a breeze off the ocean here, and tonight Hallie could feel the first chill of winter in it. Shivering in her damp nightgown, she sat down on the rock, pulled her knees up under her chin, and wrapped her arms around her legs for warmth. She stayed there, watching the water, while the brisk wind whipped her hair and the waves crashed against the rocks below her. The first elation of having helped Globo was ebbing away, and in its place, she was beginning to feel a little sad.

Globo was safe and free now, but he was gone, and so was Melae. If Globo was well, there was no reason for the two whales to come back to the harbor. She would probably never see them again. She had never said goodbye to Melae, and now maybe she would never speak to her again, never talk to her about all the things she had hoped to, never hear her glad whistling or her great gentle voice.

And there was Josh, too. Hallie had never figured out a way for Melae to speak with him, and now it was too late. When she thought of Josh, even the thrill of knowing she had helped Globo didn't take away the sting of sadness. What difference did helping Globo make, after all, when she had not been able to do anything to help her own brother when he needed her? In a jumble of confused feelings, Hallie sat shivering on the hard rock, while the sea wind kept blowing and the moon rolled down through the silver sky and the tide ebbed steadily away.

By the time the sky to the east began to lighten at last with the pink streaks of dawn, Hallie was chilled to the bone. She stood up stiffly in the pale gray light, stretching her arms over her head. A hot shower would be comforting, she thought, and maybe a steaming cup of tea with plenty of milk and sugar. She yawned, about to turn away from the water and begin the trudge toward home, when she thought she caught a glimpse of something moving, far out on the sea.

She stood still, staring toward the east, where the sky

and water glowed with rosy light. She thought she'd seen a quick gleaming blackness, a moving dot against the rose. She gazed until her eyes ached, until she saw dancing black dots everywhere she looked. Nothing. She had been staring at the water too long; that was all it was.

She turned away and took a few steps across the rock, her nose full of the rank smell of rockweed exposed by the ebbing tide. Then she stopped and looked back toward the east once more.

The red sphere of the sun was just rolling up over the edge of the world, throwing its light over the ocean, making a trail of gold across the water. And in that trail she saw, this time with no possibility of doubt, coming toward her across the water, two high, sharp fins, two black backs, two soft clouds of breath, pink in the early light.

She stood and stared. She tried to shout, but couldn't find her breath. She scrambled over Whaleback's high gray ridge, slid down onto the slick, green rocks at its foot, slipped across the seaweed and barnacles to the water's edge, yanked up her nightgown, and splashed in.

"Melae!" she cried. "Globo! Melae!"

SMALL ONE! The whale's voice rang through Hallie like a bell. Out in the deep water, well away from the rocks, the two whales swung into a circle, and the one with the shorter fin lifted her tail out of the water and splashed it against the surface, scattering a bright spray of droplets into the golden light.

"Melae, you came back!"

WE CAME TO THANK YOU, SMALL ONE. Melae's voice sang with joy, while the whale herself rose to the surface and dove and rose again, rolled her black body in the early light, lobbed her tail against the water with a glad, sharp smack. *GLOBO IS WELL, AS YOU CAN SEE. HE ASKS ME TO GIVE YOU HIS THANKS.*

"Tell him I was glad I could help." Hallie's voice shook with happiness. "It was luck, mostly. I just happened to hear him."

NOT JUST LUCK, said Melae. *YOU LISTENED, AND YOU DID WHAT YOU COULD.*

"But how did Globo know I was the one in the boat?" asked Hallie.

HE DID NOT KNOW WHO IT WAS. BUT I GUESSED.

Hallie hesitated. "But, Melae, where were you?" she asked at last. "If you knew about it, why didn't you come?"

I DID NOT KNOW UNTIL AFTER, said the whale. *OUT IN THE DEEP I COULD NOT HEAR GLOBO, COULD NOT FIND HIM. WHEN WE DID FIND EACH OTHER, HE TOLD ME HOW A SMALL SHELL HAD CHASED HIM FREE OF THE ROCKY PLACE. I GUESSED THAT THE SHELL WAS YOURS.*

Hallie shivered in the morning chill. "I'm sorry those people chased you away yesterday, Melae. I couldn't stop them."

DON'T BE SORRY, SMALL ONE. THEY DID NOT HARM US.

"They didn't want to hurt you . . . the people who chased you, I mean. They only wanted to help." Suddenly, Hallie wanted urgently to explain, to keep Melae from thinking that people were all bad, that humans meant only harm and trouble. "They thought it would help, to split you up. They didn't want to just stand by and do nothing, when you and Globo were in trouble. They were going to try to take care of Globo today, if he was still sick."

The sun had lifted itself free of the water by now, and the sky and the sea were alight with gold. In the water the two whales circled, more calmly now, their glossy backs reflecting the gold of the sun.

"Melae, now that you're here, are . . . are you going to stay?" Hallie asked cautiously.

NO, SMALL ONE, Melae said regretfully. THE SHALLOWS ARE NOT OUR HOME. WE MUST GO BACK TO THE DEEP NOW AND FIND THE OTHER SWIMMERS.

Hallie closed her eyes and nodded. After all, the whales had never belonged in the harbor. Still, she had to swallow hard before she spoke.

"We won't be able to talk anymore, will we? Because you can't hear me from so far away?"

I AM AFRAID NOT, SMALL ONE.

Hallie nodded one more time, fighting for control. "Melae, thank you for coming back," she said at last, her voice shaky again. "I was afraid you'd go away without saying good-bye, and leave me alone."

The whale's voice rippled as if with laughter. THIS STRANGE IDEA, ALONE, AGAIN, she said. SMALL ONE, THERE IS NO ALONE. ALL OF US ARE TOGETHER.

Out on the water, the two whales circled one more time, came up side by side, their two backs arching high, and dove deep beneath the golden water. The first to surface, farther off now, was Globo. He lifted his tail once and brought it down against the water in a resounding farewell smack. Then he dove again and was gone.

"Oh, don't go yet," Hallie cried. "Melae, wait."

Up through the rippling water came Melae's black back one more time, circling closer to Hallie in the deep channel off the rock. *YES, SMALL ONE.*

"Melae, what about my brother? Josh, I mean. You never got to talk to him . . . to help him."

AHH, YOUR JOSH. The whale's voice was calm and strong. *YOU DO NOT NEED MY HELP FOR HIM.*

"Oh, but, Melae . . ." Hallie began, and then she stopped herself. Out on the water, she could see the distant black spot that was Globo's fin, swimming slowly toward the east, waiting for Melae to catch up. After a minute, she spoke again, her voice trembling only a little.

"Do you think maybe you could come back here again someday? To say hello? Or maybe just to sing a little?"

The whale's voice rippled with laughter again. *I HOPE SO, SMALL ONE. SOMEDAY.*

"Maybe then Josh could hear you, or my friend Melissa," said Hallie.

I WOULD LIKE THAT, the whale said gravely.

"And, Melae, I wanted to say thank you," said Hallie. "For saving me that day, when I fell in. And for . . . well, for listening to me. For being my friend."

SMALL ONE, I THANK YOU, TOO. YOU WILL

BE IN ALL MY SONGS. Melae's voice resounded, deeper, stronger, and warmer than Hallie had ever heard it before. Then, out on the water, the whale circled once more and dove. Hallie caught her breath. Melae's words had sounded like a farewell. Don't go, Hallie wanted to cry. I'm not ready yet.

But then the whale burst once more through the waves, her gleaming black head rising straight out of the water, so that Hallie could see the bulge of her forehead, the small eyes set wide on either side of her head, the smiling curve of her mouth, the two short flippers, and even a surprising gleam of white on her belly. Hallie's breath stopped in her throat. For a brief second, Melae seemed to look straight into Hallie's eyes. Hallie raised one hand above her head in a salute. Then Melae dropped back into the water with a splash, flicked her tail once, turned toward the east, and dove.

As soon as she disappeared beneath the waves, Melae began to whistle. The glad, wild fluting echoed through Hallie's bones, and she stood in the water listening, watching for the glossy fin that emerged now and then beyond the breakers, farther away each time, until it joined Globo's and they disappeared together into the glinting light of the eastern sea.

The singing took longer to fade away. The sun rose higher and the morning gathered light as Hallie stood in the water, listening to Melae's farewell music. Gulls wheeled overhead, searching for breakfast, and a flock of ducks flapped down out of the sky to bob beyond the breakers. Hallie could no longer catch even a glimpse of distant black fins.

But still the whistling sounded through her bones, and still she stood, ankle-deep in the gentle waves, until she could hear the whale's song only in her memory. Not until then did she turn away from the water and start at last on her cold, bare feet across the weed-slicked rocks toward home.

By the time the first Sunday morning ferry left the island a few hours later, rain clouds had rolled across the sky from the northwest. A gray quiet muffled the harbor as the boat chugged slowly across the still water.

There were few passengers on the ferry so early on a Sunday morning. Hallie sat alone in the bow, watching the foamy white ruffle of the wake sweep up from the gray water, thinking how strange it felt not to be listening for Melae. She heard the everyday music of the harbor, the wind singing past her ears, the deep throb of the ferry engine, the endless crying of gulls. But in her memory, she also heard Melae's voice. YOU LISTENED, the whale had told her. YOU DID WHAT YOU COULD.

Rain began to spatter down from the dull, gray sky. It pattered on the steel deck and hissed softly into the sea, dimpling the water's surface into countless interlocking circles. The rain was cool and gentle on Hallie's tired head and shoulders. She lifted her face to its softness and closed her eyes.

"Hey," said somebody beside her. "I've heard about not knowing enough to come in out of the rain. But I thought I was the only dumb one."

She opened her eyes and there stood Ira, smiling at her from under the damp brim of his red deckhand cap.

"Want this to keep the rain off your head?" He took off the billed cap and held it out toward her.

"No, thanks," she said, smiling at him. "I kind of like the rain."

"Okay, if you say so." Ira set down a coil of rope and leaned against the deck rail, letting the rain fall on his curly hair. For a moment they were both quiet, watching the wet docks slip closer as the ferry glided toward the city.

"Hey, Ira, I brought these back." Hallie fished in her pack and pulled out his flip-flops. "And here's the ticket I owe you, too. Thanks for helping me the other day."

"Oh, that's okay." He took them and looked at her soberly. "It wasn't much to do, but I've been wanting to help out somehow, ever since your brother got hurt. It's strange not to have the little guy around, pestering us with questions and wanting to help with the freight the way he always does."

"It feels strange to me, too," said Hallie.

"How is he, anyway?" asked Ira.

"I don't exactly know," said Hallie. "He's getting better, my parents say. But I haven't seen him since he got hurt. I'm . . . well, I'm on my way to the hospital to visit him right now." It was the first time she had admitted it, even to herself.

"You are? Well, here." He handed her the red cap, with its Garnet Island Ferry District logo. "Give him this from me, would you?"

Hallie took it. "Oh, he'll love it! But, Ira, you need this, don't you? Are you sure you want to give it away?"

"Sure I'm sure." Ira grinned down at her. "A person's

got to do what they can, you know. Even if it's just some dumb little thing."

Hallie stood in the gentle rain, turning the cap over and over in her fingers. Ira's words echoed strangely in her mind. For a moment she thought she had heard Melae's voice again.

"I know what you mean," she said finally, smiling up at Ira. "That's what I think, too."

The chug of the engine slowed suddenly as the ferry steamed toward the landing ramp, and Ira glanced back at the stern. "Well, I've got to get back to work," he said. "Tell Josh hi for me, okay?"

"I will," said Hallie. "Thanks again for the hat. And for the flip-flops, too," she called after Ira as he loped down the steps to the rear deck. Then she leaned on the rail, gazing down at the quiet, rain-pocked surface of the harbor, until the ferry docked and it was time to get off.

14

The rain stopped as Hallie walked up the pier from the boat landing. Waterfront Street was empty of traffic. The boutiques were closed on Sunday mornings, and the tourists were still asleep in their hotels. The city was quiet as Hallie splashed through the wet streets, climbing Lighthouse Hill.

At the hospital, she paused just inside the big glass lobby doors. A few people sat uneasily in hard orange plastic chairs, leafing through out-of-date magazines without really reading them. Dim light fell from the windows onto their tired faces and onto the dusty plastic plants and bare linoleum. Only the occasional squall of a baby or the blare of a garbled message on the loudspeaker broke the quiet.

Hallie had been in the lobby before, but she had never gone beyond it. She knew from her visit to the parking lot with her mother that Josh's room was on the second floor at the end of the building nearest to the water. But she didn't know how to get there, or what his room number was, and she was afraid to ask anyone. She didn't want to be stopped because she was too young to visit. Of course, she could always lie and say that she was twelve. She'd do that if she had to. But she hoped she could just find Josh's room by herself.

First, she had to get past the reception desk. Although she had worried about how to manage this on the way over, it turned out to be easy. By luck, a group of people who seemed to be members of one large family came in right after Hallie, loaded down with flowers and presents wrapped in baby paper. Hallie drew herself up, hoping that she could pass for at least thirteen, and crossed the lobby close behind them, trying to look like a part of their family. She let herself be swept along with the laughing group past the reception desk and the security guard, into a long hallway that led to a bank of elevators.

An elevator car had just arrived, its doors sliding silently open. The family crowded into the car, and Hallie went with them. She stood pressed into a corner with a bunch of yellow gladioli tickling her nose, while the family talked and joked about the new baby they had come to see. The car rose with a lurch to the second floor, where everyone spilled out of the car again.

Behind the high counter of a nursing station by the second-floor elevator door, a nurse was talking on the phone with his back turned. Another nurse glanced away from a computer screen just long enough to direct the family Hallie had joined to the maternity wing, down the hallway to the right. The nurse turned back to the computer without watching them go, and so she didn't notice when Hallie lagged behind. Wherever Josh was, she was sure his room wasn't in the maternity wing.

But where was he? Long hallways stretched away on

both sides of the nursing station and straight ahead, and other corridors branched off in the shadowy distances. People bustled through the halls, doctors and nurses in crisp white, orderlies in pale blue uniforms carrying mop buckets, patients in slippers and robes, visitors in ordinary clothes, all looking as if they knew exactly where they were going. Nobody seemed to notice Hallie standing by the elevator, uncertain and alone.

Although the hospital was the largest building in the city, until this moment Hallie had not quite realized just how big it was. Which of these hallways led to Josh? Hallie tried to remember where she and her mother had stood, the day Josh had waved down to her from his window. Where had they been? In the windowless interior of the hospital, she was disoriented and confused.

But if she stood here looking lost much longer, somebody was going to notice her. At random, she picked the hall straight ahead and started down it, her sneakered feet squeaking on the polished brown linoleum. The hallway smelled of disinfectant, floor wax, and overcooked cabbage. There were other smells, too, faint and unpleasant, that Hallie found she didn't want to recognize.

The plastered walls, lined with doors, were painted a dull green. Why did they pick such a sad color, Hallie wondered as she walked, instead of something that would cheer up people? She found herself staring through an open door into the face of the person lying inside, a pale face so wrinkled under its short tufts of white hair that Hallie couldn't tell if it belonged to a man or a woman, staring back at her out of hollowed dark eyes like holes. Embarrassed, she yanked her gaze away and hurried on.

The next door was half-open, and all she could see beyond it was a pair of legs exposed on wrinkled sheets. The legs were old, skinny, and bluish. Clearly they didn't belong to anyone as young as Josh. Grateful that she couldn't see the face that went with them, Hallie glanced across the hall.

There, a door stood wide open. Inside, a woman with rough, uncombed hair lay with her back to the door, so that Hallie couldn't help seeing the bare knobs of her spine, exposed by the hospital gown's open back.

She turned away, dismayed. This was the wrong part of the hospital. Where was the children's section? Where was Josh? Hallie stood still for a moment. For the first time since her decision to visit Josh had made itself in her heart as Melae had swum away into the golden sunrise, she felt a stab of doubt. What if she couldn't find him? What if, even if she did, she couldn't recognize him? What did her brother look like, anyway? All of a sudden, she couldn't seem to remember his face.

She closed her eyes in panic for a minute. What was she doing here? Why had she ever thought she could sneak into this giant place and find her brother, all by herself?

"Excuse me, please, miss."

Hallie opened her eyes and stepped quickly out of the path of an orderly pushing a clanking cart loaded with covered trays. For the first time she noticed a sign on the wall, with an arrow pointing down the hall in the direction the orderly was pushing the cart. It read PEDI-

ATRICS. That meant children. Hadn't her mother said that was where Josh had been moved?

Hallie followed the orderly's pale blue back down the long hallway, past more doors that she avoided looking through, around a corner under another PEDIATRICS sign, through swinging double doors into another corridor. The walls here were yellow, and in an effort to make them more cheerful, they had been painted with cartoon murals. But the paint was faded now and the murals were beginning to chip, so that the effect was not much more cheerful than the plain, dull green.

The orderly pushed his cart into the first room on the left. "Morning, honey," he said gently. "Breakfast time." Hallie peered through the door. A bed with tall steel bars, like a giant crib, stood inside, and a toddler, a little boy with a tangle of black hair who looked about two, sat in the bed, holding on to the bars. The orderly reached over and ruffled the curls on the top of the little boy's head before he took a tray off his cart.

The gentleness of his gesture made Hallie feel a little better, and she started down the hall toward the next door. But before she got close enough to look in, a high, loud, little-boy voice broke the quiet of the hallway, shouting cheerfully. At the end of the hall, with a bright window behind him so that all she could see was vague outlines, a small boy in a wheelchair was zipping around in circles, pivoting on one wheel like a stunt-car driver. One leg, wrapped in white, stuck out stiffly from the chair, propped on a leg rest. The boy was so lively that he shattered the quiet of the hallway like a blast of rock and roll. As Hallie watched, a shaft of light caught his hair. It glinted bright red.

"Josh? Josh!" Hallie ran down the hall, gasping with relief. He couldn't be as badly hurt as she had feared, after all, if he could zip around in a wheelchair like this. As she ran, the boy tilted the chair onto its rear wheels, spun out of his circle and whizzed toward her, pushing his wheels with fast, energetic shoves. Hallie had almost reached him when she stopped short.

The boy was not Josh. His red hair stuck up straight, instead of falling into a mess of curls the way her brother's did, and he was seven or eight, older than Josh. His glance traveled past Hallie without recognition as he wheeled past the spot where she stood frozen in disappointment, and she saw that his leg was not bandaged, as Josh's probably was, but set into a plaster cast.

She swallowed her dismay, shook herself out of her frozenness, and called after him. "Hey, wait a minute. Do you know a boy in this hospital called Josh Rainsford?"

The boy barely paused. "Nope," he threw over his shoulder. "Never heard of him. Want to sign my cast?"

"Um, not right now, thanks," Hallie said. The boy pivoted his chair again, wheeled through one of the open doors, and disappeared.

Hallie stood by the windows at the end of the hall, so disappointed that for a moment she could hardly move. Somewhere a child was crying, in a thin, high voice like a sea gull's. Hallie wished she could close her ears.

Maybe Mom was right after all, she thought. Maybe I shouldn't have come.

Then, from one of the open doorways, a nurse in a white pantsuit emerged. Hallie backed into the corner, where the window curtains half hid her from the nurse's view, but the nurse wasn't looking at her. Her dark head was bent toward a small girl in a hospital gown who walked uncertainly beside her, taking slow, shaky steps. The nurse had one armed wrapped protectively around the child's shoulders.

"Okay, now, let's just walk a little way," Hallie heard the nurse say softly, as the two walked slowly up the hall away from Hallie. "I know it's tough, but I'll help you. You can do it."

Something about the nurse was familiar; something in the softness of her voice, or the attentive curve of her brown neck above the white uniform, reminded Hallie so sharply of somebody that unexpected tears stung in her eyes. Was it Mrs. Gianopoulos she was thinking of, or her own mother? Or was it Melae?

She turned to the window behind her, blinking back her tears. Maybe this isn't such an awful place, she thought. After all, they're just trying to help people here.

From the window, she could see the ocean beyond the city rooftops, spread out under the cloudy sky like a sheet of wrinkled, silver silk. Garnet Island lay in the harbor, surrounded by a white frill of surf, the long arm of Whaleback reaching out across the channel toward Tourmaline. It felt strange to see her home from up here, so small and complete, as if she were looking down at her whole life.

She could see the ferry, a small spot of red and yellow chugging across the harbor. Ira was down there on the ferry, and Melissa was on the island, and Mr. and Mrs. Gianopoulos, and everybody else she knew. And so was Hallie's house, her room, her father's books, Josh's toys, and sitting on top of her mother's piano, the picture of all four of them, together on the beach on Josh's birthday, laughing.

She had never thought about it before, but from here she could see how the Jewel Islands, Garnet and Tourmaline and Ruby, lay together in one curving crescent, as if they were all part of the same undersea ridge. They aren't really islands at all, she thought suddenly. They're all part of one pattern. They're connected to each other.

And beyond the islands, in that great sweep of gray ocean, Melae and Globo were out there somewhere, whistling their wild whale music. Maybe they had found the other pilot whales by now, and they were all swimming together.

Then, for just a moment, as strongly as if she could still hear her, Hallie felt the comfort of Melae's presence flooding through her like the warmth of the sun on a summer day.

SMALL ONE, Melae would say if she could, in her great, gentle, musical voice, half laughing at Hallie for needing to be reminded. Hallie could hear her almost as clearly as if the whale really were speaking to her. SMALL ONE, THERE IS NO ALONE, REMEMBER? WE ARE ALL TOGETHER.

Smiling in spite of herself, Hallie pulled her eyes away from the gray rim of the sea. And that was when she saw, for the first time, that the parking lot beneath the window where she stood was familiar, that she was standing above the same patch of grass, with its lone sapling and wilting geraniums, where she had stood a few days before, waving up at Josh's window.

She had found Josh after all. His room must be right here, at the end of this hallway. She turned from the window to the closed door across the hall. But as she did, the door swung open, and from it emerged her mother and father.

They stopped short, staring at her. Nobody said anything for a moment, but her father pulled the door quietly shut behind him.

It was Hallie who spoke first. "Hi, Mom. Hi, Dad," she said steadily. "I'm here to see Josh."

Her mother's brows pulled into a frown. "Hallie, dear, we've already discussed this," she began, but Hallie's father interrupted. He was looking straight at Hallie.

"Wait, Helen," he said. "Wait. Let's listen first."

"I have to." Hallie spoke calmly to her mother. "I need to be with Josh. Don't you see?"

Her father was nodding, but her mother's face was creased with doubt.

"I know you want to protect me, Mom," said Hallie. "But I'm older than you think. I need Josh, and Josh needs me."

Her mother opened her mouth as if to argue, looked at Hallie, looked at Hallie's father, closed her mouth again. "Well," she said at last. "Maybe I didn't realize how much it means to you. Maybe I was wrong. He misses you, I know that."

Hallie's father put an arm around her mother's shoulders, and they leaned against each other.

"So, can I go in?" Hallie looked from one face to the other.

"Go ahead, honey." Her father patted Hallie's shoulder. "You picked a good day for it. He's awake, and he's feeling pretty good this morning. The doctors are even talking about sending him home for a while later this week, until he's ready for the skin grafts. Go ahead in."

"Is it okay if I go by myself?" All of a sudden Hallie felt doubtful.

"Go ahead, Hallie. We'll come in a few minutes," her mother said, and her parents stepped away from the door.

Hallie took a deep breath and turned away from her parents' tired, loving faces. As surely as if she had passed through it many times before, she crossed the hall, pushed the door open, and walked into her brother's room.

Josh was alone, small in the big bed with a white sheet propped above his legs like a tent. He didn't see Hallie at first; his face was turned toward the window. His profile was sharper than Hallie remembered, his freckles standing out more clearly than they used to, his summer tan all gone. There was a faint, unfamiliar smell in the air, of medicine and disinfectant.

"Josh?" she whispered uncertainly. But when he turned to her and she saw his small face with the gray eyes just like her mother's, just like her own, her doubts vanished.

His surprised grin showed the gap where the tooth

had fallen out on his birthday, partly filled by the new one. It took Hallie two steps to cross the room and put her arms around him.

"Josh, I missed you," she said into his red curly hair.

"Hah. I didn't miss you one bit," he said, but his wiry arms, wrapped tight around her neck, told her the truth. She pulled back, smiled at him, and crossed her eyes.

He stuck his tongue out at her, the way he always had, and then went back to grinning, as if he couldn't help it. "Mom and Dad didn't tell me you were coming. I thought you weren't supposed to."

"They didn't know I was coming," admitted Hallie. "I snuck in. But I met them outside, and they said it was okay."

"They were going down to the cafeteria to get some breakfast. I just had mine." Josh gestured at a tray full of dishes on his bedside table. "Soft-boiled eggs and soggy toast. Yuck. Did you bring anything to eat?"

His glance at her backpack was so hopeful that Hallie couldn't help laughing. "No, sorry," she said. "But, you know what, I do have a present for you in here."

She reached into her pack and pulled out Ira's cap, a little grubby and still slightly damp. She set it on Josh's head. It was so big that it settled down over his eyes, covering all but his freckled cheeks and his grin.

"Wow! Just like Ira's," he said from under the hat.

"It *is* Ira's. He sent it to you."

"It's Ira's? Really?" Josh's grin disappeared, and he reached up reverently to touch the cap. Then he pushed it gently back so that the bill pointed at the ceiling and his eyes showed again. This time, Hallie noticed the dark shadows under them, like bruises.

"Um . . ." Hallie hesitated a moment, then plunged on. "How is your leg, Josh? I mean, how do you feel?"

Josh glanced down briefly, almost in irritation, at the white tent of sheet hiding his legs. "It's better, I guess," he said. "It still hurts. But I can walk a little now."

Hallie twisted at the hem of his sheet. "Josh, I . . . I wish I had helped more. I kind of panicked, I guess, that day. I mean, the day you got hurt. I'm sorry."

Josh looked up at her in surprise. "But you did help."

"No, I didn't, I just stood there," Hallie began automatically, but Josh kept talking, his eyes a little shadowed with remembering.

"Everybody else was running around yelling, but you were real quiet and calm. You just stayed with me and held my hand. I was glad you were there," he said matter-of-factly. "Do you think you could maybe bring me a doughnut, next time you come? Maybe even two doughnuts? They never have doughnuts here."

Hallie laughed out loud in mingled surprise and relief. "Well, sure. I'll bring you a bagful of doughnuts," she said.

"Chocolate ones?" he asked wistfully.

"Chocolate with frosting *and* sprinkles," she promised. "Your favorites."

"Okay, then." Josh settled back against his pillow, as if something important had been settled.

Hallie sat down carefully on the edge of the bed beside him, trying not to joggle his hurt leg under the sheet. She put an arm around her brother, and his small body relaxed against hers. It was beginning to rain again. She could hear it spattering against the window.

After a moment, she said, "I've got something to tell you, Joshie. Remember the secret I told you about, on the phone? It's about the whales in the harbor."

As Josh nodded, Ira's cap slipped forward over his eyes. "Dad told me about them. I could see them from up here, sometimes, with his binoculars."

"Well, they're gone now. But there's part of the story Dad didn't tell you, because he didn't know about it. Nobody knows but me."

Before she could say any more, the doorknob clicked and the door swung open.

"Here come Mom and Dad. I'll tell you later," whispered Hallie quickly.

"You better," Josh whispered back. He stuck out his tongue at her, and she crossed her eyes at him. And then their parents came toward them, smiling. Outside the small, lighted, golden island of Josh's room, the rain fell on the hospital, on the city, on the harbor and the islands and the ocean. And somewhere, far away under the gray waves, the whales swam, singing, through the sea.